ALONE

Lin Weich

Produced by:

FriesenPress
Suite 300 – 852 Fort Street
Victoria, BC, Canada V8W 1H8

www.friesenpress.com

Distributed to the trade by The Ingram Book Company

Acknowledgements

I AM INDEBTED TO THE FOLLOWING PEOPLE FOR THEIR EFFORTS and contributions to my third novel, *Alone*.

My thanks to Jeff Dinsdale and Denise Harris for sharing their expertise and knowledge about anxiety disorders; Ed Zaruk for sharing his wealth of information about Beaver aircraft; Dennis for all your assistance; Pat Marshall, Chris Clark and Marian Zaruk for their many hours spent editing and proofreading; Margaret Pascuzzo for proofreading.

Special thanks to my husband Brian, my family and friends who encourage me to follow my dreams.

ALSO BY LIN WEICH

Strength of an Eagle (2012)
Half-Truths, Total Lies (2012)

ALONE

Lin Weich

Chapter 1

HER CALVES BURNED AS SHE FLED DOWN THE CONCRETE STAIRS. Slipping on decaying leaves, she vanished into a dismal, half-lit stairwell. Mary breathed slowly through narrowed lips, trying to slow her racing heart. They were coming.

"Down here! Down here!"

"Where?"

"For God's sake, hurry up, Sharon! The little bitch will get away again."

Panting breaths and the quiet slaps of sneakered feet confirmed their progress into the depths of the underground space. With hands smothering giggles, her pursuers searched the gloom. Wafts of cheap perfume and garlic permeated the stairwell.

She held her breath. Silent moments hung eternally; a snicker pulsated in the fetid atmosphere.

"Hey, look who's here. Waiting for us?"

Dread, fear and panic drained her of any means of escape. The coarse pebbled wall grazed her lower back as Mary slumped against it. "Please, please," she begged as they reached through the damp grabbing her sweatshirt, spinning her around.

Struggling against the arms that held hers tightly in a knot behind her back, she leaned helplessly away from the stinging slaps bouncing off her cheeks. First, the normal side of her face, hurt. Then the other, the more sensitive birth-marked cheek that made her so different, flamed in response. Closing her eyes against the pain and to the tears that threatened to spurt like coward's milk, she suffered another beating. The physical injuries, however, were no match for the caustic venom issuing from their taunting mouths. "Half-faced bitch, ying-yang, cow-face." Now, just like every day, she braved the cruel demeaning shouts and taunts hurled in her direction. Unable to stop hopeless tears from coursing her ugly face, Mary endured the gang's abuse.

◇◇◇◇◇◇

As the afternoon bell shrieked, carefree high school students flowed noisily through the halls. Sara scanned the laughing, jostling mob. There was no trace of Mary in the endless sea of faces. Troubled, she turned in the direction of her next class.

The drone of Mr. Watson's mind-numbing statistics lesson competed with her gut feeling that something was really wrong this time. Sure, Mary sometimes stayed late at her previous class. Often she avoided her bullies by skipping classes, but no, the world had tilted. Something was wrong. Carelessly scraping her chair across gritty linoleum, Sara bolted out of the room.

She checked the library, Mary's last classroom, the medical room, the office and finally Mary's locker. She saw a faded, blue gym bag splayed open inside the narrow space. Lunch spilled from it. Mary's purse hung from a hook inside the door. She would not have gone home or skipped class without taking her purse.

Another bell rang and another stream of students pushed towards the last class of the day. Beside the bulletin board, she saw a group of Mary's enemies huddled in secret whisperings.

They noticed her staring and quickly looked away. Guilt was etched on their faces. Defensiveness stiffened their posture. Silently, the group melted into the student body.

◇◇◇◇◇◇◇

At three-thirty, Sharon crossed the lobby and ran down the hall towards her locker. Late for practice, she didn't notice Sara until it was too late.

She flinched as Sara shoved her up against the metal lockers.

"Not so tough without your buddies are you?" Sara hissed into the delicate oval of her ear. "Where is Mary? What have you done to her?"

Sharon felt the blood drain from her face.

Sara took the opportunity to slam her against the locker again. "Where is Mary?"

Sharon glanced anxiously around, looking for her posse. Emptiness echoed off steel storage units. No one was coming to her rescue any time soon. "We left her in the stairwell next to the gym exit. We didn't touch her. We found her beat up, but she wouldn't come with us. She was afraid. She's probably still there, the little two-faced cow." Sharon spat out the words as she pushed against Sara's grip. Freeing herself, she turned and sneered. "Wait till I tell Mr. Watson on you. Attacking me in school. Your sorry ass will be expelled. Watson is my Dad's best friend, you know."

◇◇◇◇◇◇◇

"Shh, shhh, I'm here now," whispered Sara as she held her sister. "You're safe with me. I'll always look after you. Come on. Let's get you home."

CHAPTER 2

THE JOURNEY TO THEIR NEW LIFE ON THE ISOLATED WEST COAST
had been long, filled with drama and uncertainty. While it had
begun with their father Sam, eventually, all the family became
willing and eager participants in this adventure into self-sufficiency.

Sam could easily remember when his dream of wilderness life
became a reality. He had been slouched in his usual seat on the
diesel fumed bus staring out of the smog streaked window, wishing
for clean air. As he fought the rising urge to scream at the noise,
pollution and crowds, he knew in his core that there must be a
better place. Images of sunlit streams trickling down rough, worn
cliffs and emptying into gentle ocean waves that lapped at pebbled
beaches combined with the imagined odours of salt, seaweed
and spruce, vying for space in his consciousness. Those peaceful
images won.

That night as he opened the apartment door he was confronted
with the sight of Mary wrapped up securely in a blanket on the
couch beside the sterile, imitation fireplace. Sara glanced up as he
shucked his city shoes and slid his tired feet into the worn mocca-
sins he favoured. "What gives?" he asked quietly. "More trouble at
school?" The gas flames reflected in Mary's vacant eyes. Sara gently
rocked her sister trying to soothe the whimpering creature.

Anna opened the front door. Carefully, the worried parents questioned the two girls. Gradually, the whole sordid story unfolded.

Sam spoke fervently to Anna that night. "There has to be more to life than this," he said as he stroked her hair. "A man can't breathe in this godforsaken city. We live like sardines crushed in a rusty can. Just imagine a life away from the noise, dirt and smog. One where we would be able to stretch and grow. Somewhere we might call our own…a little piece of paradise."

Anna looked at her husband. They had been down this path before but for the first time, in a long while, she really looked at him. Fatigue and stress had begun to etch more wrinkles into those once smooth cheeks. It had been so long since she had seen him walk with purpose. These days, his stooped shoulders, reflected his growing sorrow. When Sam succumbed to depression he often yielded to pressures of drugs or alcohol. Now that they had the girls, that would be disastrous. Their daughters were her top priority and needed the presence of both parents in their lives. "I know you are unhappy, but we can't just leave. Where would we go? Where would you get another job that pays as well as Nooms?" she asked quietly.

Sam moved further away from her on the couch. His voice came muffled from his hands cupping his face. "We would be okay. Life is a gamble. For God's sake and ours, let's roll that dice." New determination brightened his eyes. "Come on, Anna; let's live; not just exist."

Anna took a deep breath and smiled. "Okay. I'm willing to make some changes, but they have to be thought out. The girls need to go to school. You have to get another job somewhere. We can't live on thin air. We need a plan."

"School," he shouted. "School. Mary can't take any more of this abuse. We can't protect her. Look at the state she was in tonight. Like a friggin' zombie."

"Shh, don't shout," Anna pleaded. "She finally fell asleep upstairs. I know she can't take it. Tomorrow will be another round of tears and stomach aches; anything to get out of going to school."

"Nothing has changed since we spoke to Mr. Watson. The bullying continues, and I'm not at all sure the education they are getting is worth all the nastiness. You have your degree. You know how to teach. You could homeschool them or do that distance education thing I read about in the *Times*." He spoke quickly, plans and ideas swirling in his head.

Snatching a creased map from the catch all basket, he gestured wildly.

"Here, give me that pen. You get to pick where we go ...so long as it isn't a God damn city," he said spreading the map flat on the kitchen table. "Close your eyes."

With those words, he twirled his wife and encouraged her to stab in the direction of the crinkled paper. The pen landed roughly six miles off the isolated coast in the northern portion of the province. It was the middle of nowhere.

"Oh my God," exclaimed Anna as she realized where they had chosen. "There is nothing there but rocks, ocean and wilderness."

"Exactly, couldn't be better."

"No, it is miles from civilization. How would we get help if something happened?" Anna asked, fear echoing in her voice.

"Haven't you heard of the Coast Guard? We'd have a radio or satellite phone for emergencies. More could happen right here. There was that rape in the Hillside Apartments just last month. Next door was broken into in June. Those things won't be a concern for us anymore. Besides, we'll know what to do. We'll gain as much knowledge and expertise as possible before we go," shouted Sam excitedly.

"Shh. Keep your voice down," Anna warned again. "We don't need to tell Sara and Mary until it is decided."

"Tell us what?" The girls stood at the foot of the stairs with their eyes riveted on their parents. "Tell us what?" Mary repeated.

Sam grabbed Mary swinging her up in his arms. Her blonde hair arched in the hall light. As he kissed her purple blotched cheek, Sam was even more convinced that they were doing the right thing. He could save this gentle child. He could protect her as a father should.

Glancing over at his wife, he declared, "We are leaving this damn city. We are going to homestead like the pioneers. Just think, no more Third Street Secondary, no more polluted buses, no more noisy neighbours, no more troubles. We will be free to do whatever we want. Pioneers growing our own food, building a cabin, being a real family…a pioneer family. We are going to paradise."

◇◇◇◇◇◇

Later that night, Sara heard soft muffled sobs coming from the pile of blankets on Mary's bed. She crept over to her. "Do you want me to get in beside you?" she asked quietly. "I'll stay until you get off to sleep." She was rewarded with a tentative hand reaching out from the quilted cocoon.

"I'm such a baby, Sara. Such a baby." Dissolving into shuddering sobs, Mary clutched Sara's arm pulling her into bed.

"Oh, never you mind, never you mind. Today was really awful… today was terrible." Stroking Mary's tangled hair with her fingers; she tried to smooth the damp mess. Sweat and tears made that task impossible. They would have to get up early the next morning to shower before school. It was already past midnight. Maybe they wouldn't even have to go to school tomorrow, if what Dad said was true. They were going to move!

"Shh, Mary," she whispered, "It's okay. We're moving. Dad said somewhere on the West Coast. The kids might be nicer there. There might not even be a school nearby. Then we won't have to worry about the bullying. I think things are going to get better…it might take a little time but things are going to be alright. Shh, shh."

Eventually, Mary relaxed and fell asleep still holding on to her sister.

Sara eased herself from the now loosened grip; rose and stood by the narrow shuttered window. She opened the blind slightly. Peering out between the buildings, she paused staring down at the slice of sidewalk in front of their apartment building. The tap, tap, tap of Mr. Morgan's walking stick, echoed in her ears as he hurried along in the early morning hour. His coat, billowing from his shoulders like a crusader's cape, swept along behind him in a swirl of grey and mist. The early dawn drew long, dark shadows as he passed by the bakery.

Drawing her easel and paints from under her bed, Sara quietly set up and began to paint the background with soft, broad brush strokes. Hints of blues, greys and charcoals randomly filled the canvas, highlighting the advent of a new day. Then wielding her heavy carpenter's pencil she quickly imparted Mr. Morgan's movement as he went to fulfill his promises. Sara's artistry was unique. Several of her teachers had remarked on her considerable talent and were encouraging her to further her studies at the Academy of Fine Arts in Toronto.

◇◇◇◇◇◇◇

As Sara committed the scene to canvas, her father, Sam, watched from the doorway. He felt a twinge of guilt. If they left for parts unknown, Sara would not be going to the Academy. She wouldn't be going anywhere. Crossing over to Sara, he gently put his hand on her shoulder and turned her to face him. "Am I being unfair to you, Sara? If we leave now, just before your graduation, you will miss out on a lot. No prom, no grad, no going on to the Academy next year. We might be able to send you later, but I will need you in the beginning."

"Dad," Sara said softly. "Look at her…just look. We must to go. Nothing has worked to stop the bullying. You've tried just about everything. It was the same in the other schools. Mary can't take any more…she can't." She moved over to the window. Sam joined her and together they gazed at the city landscape.

She slipped her arm around her father's waist. "We have to go. So long as I have my paints, my family and my dreams, I will be okay. Mary has nothing but grief and heartache. We have to go." With that, the deed was done.

The Lindholm household became a flurry of frantic activity. Now that the decision was made, the family was anxious to get going. Everyone immersed themselves into researching farming methods, solar power, building techniques, first aid scenarios, animal husbandry and the like. Self-sufficiency books were collected on these topics and experts were consulted. The farm collective, down in

Marlin, proved to be a treasure trove of information on small farms and living off the land.

Anna and Sam put the small two bedroom apartment on the market. Inside a month, it was sold. After moving in with Mabel, Anna's mother, they began to liquidate their other assets.

Anna was surprised at the amount of equity they had. Mabel persuaded them to put most of the money into term deposits and trust funds, for each of the girls. "It would be a safety net, in case something goes wrong. That way you won't be left with nothing. You have the girls to think about. One or both of them might want to go to university or into a trade. I know you were thinking of the Academy for Sara. I'd hate to think that their futures might be limited by your dreams of utopia," Mabel said earnestly, as they sat gathered around her kitchen table.

"I thought you were all for us and our adventure," murmured Sam as he scrutinized the grey-haired woman.

"I am. If I were twenty years younger, I'd jump at a chance to join you on this venture. I would however, have a back-up plan. Besides, I would feel better knowing the girls would be taken care of if anything were to happen to you out there."

She made a good point and Anna promised they would visit the bank manager in the morning.

Anna picked up the *Buy & Sell* from the table. "Sam. Here's a reasonably priced boat. Is that the size we need?"

"It's in Rupert. Doesn't look bad," Sam agreed. "Mabel, do you feel like taking care of the girls for the weekend? Anna and I could fly up and have a look around. Might even get a line on some property."

CHAPTER 3

AS KARL'S EYES FOLLOWED THE MORPHINE DRIPPING DOWN THE IV tube easing his father into blessed oblivion, he wondered how much longer it would be before he was officially an orphan. Mom had died years ago on that lonely, desolate island. Cancer had taken her; leaving a heartsick husband and himself partying away his college fund. Karl resented his father. Hearing the soft moans from the nearly comatose old man, he glanced at his frail parent. He scarcely recognized the once hale and hearty pioneer who had spent decades in the bush.

"Should've been you, not Mom," he whispered. Yes, he blamed his father. If he hadn't dragged his family off to the West Coast, she might still be alive. His father and his brother Sven should have stayed put after they hit pay dirt in the Yukon. But no, they had purchased that pre-emption and moved the four of them to the middle of nowhere. Not that Uncle Sven had any other family to bring. For as long as Karl could remember, he had been a crusty old bachelor.

Another moan from the bed and his father weakly raised his head. "Sven, Sven…I'm sorry…sorry."

The lonely old man had tried to make amends before he'd moved back to the town, but Sven had stubbornly spurned his overtures.

Sven had no use for his brother. Harry had caught Sonja and him making love in the cave that the family used for cold storage. They had been so involved that they hadn't even heard his approach. A shocked and devastated Harry had driven them away. Sven firmly believed the ensuing grief and stress had led to Sonja's illness and her death.

Harry had given Sonja just a day to make the hardest decision of her life. Sven or Karl. She had been faced with an impossible choice. They could not continue to live at the homestead. She could not give up the love of her life. After making Harry promise that Karl would be free to visit, Sonja chose to leave her nearly grown-up son with his father.

Sven took one of the boats, enough food to last Sonja and him until the spring seas calmed, the old army tent, some equipment and the wad of money Harry had chucked in his face. He signed a hastily drawn-up paper that cut all ties and obligations between his brother and him. Sven set up his own cabin on the distant island that marked the entrance to their bay; choosing to face the cabin towards the open ocean, avoiding the sight of the old homestead. He never spoke of or to his brother again.

Harry turned inward in his despair. He seldom spoke to his son and went about his daily life in gruff silence. Karl was desolate. He missed his mother terribly and couldn't understand why she had left him alone with this shell of a man. As soon as he turned eighteen, he left the island; turning his back on his childhood home and the man who was his father in name only. Karl never visited his mother while she was on the island with Sven. His heart ached, but he couldn't bring himself to cross the channel to the island camp. She had chosen Sven. She had abandoned him. That was unforgivable.

The grief of losing her only son tore Sonja apart. When the cancer struck, guilt and regret took over. She didn't even fight the insidious disease.

Uncle Sven still lived on that island opposite his father's isolated homestead. The island was part of the pre-emption, but several miles of ocean and many empty years separated the brothers. The once close siblings were destined never to reconcile. Now time had run out, and Harry would be dead before long.

Karl let his thoughts drift again. The brothers had been very well off, especially after the bonanza. Both were not spenders. Once the cabins had been built, supplies for the homestead could not have eaten into their savings very much. Yes, there was probably a fortune to be had. For sure, the money was not stashed in a bank. The old timers had set no store in banks; preferring to have their cash close at hand. Cash was the currency of the bush. Their mattresses must be stuffed with mouldy dollar bills.

"Sven, Sonja…sorry." The sound of desperation, of sorrow and of supplication filled every corner of the silent room.

Then, nothing. Karl looked up and knew his father had gone.

Karl crossed over to the door and looked towards the nursing station. Quiet laughter drifted on the hospital's stale air. The whirring of the oxygen machine filled the room behind him. With a tentative step, he advanced on the group of nurses. "Ah, excuse me," he said as the pretty nurse looked up. "I think it's over. What do I do now?"

Suddenly, all business, the nurses went into action. As he watched, they shut off all the equipment, unhooked the tubes and lines from his father's body and gazed sympathetically at Karl. "Do you want a few more moments before we take him downstairs?"

Fed up with the long vigil, the hospital stench, and the pretence of caring, Karl scowled. "No, take him away…he's been gone from my life forever. This is merely the last hurrah."

Used to all sorts of reactions to death, the nurses simply pulled up the sheet and began to wheel his father from the room. "Come to the station and we will release his effects. You can call the hospital morgue to make arrangements for your father's remains, once you have everything in place. You have three days to decide."

Clacking wheels masked the soft padding of the nurses' soles. With them went the only reason to stay in this germ infested, carbolic atmosphere. Hardly able to stand another claustrophobic minute on the ward, he stood and glanced around. When his time came he hoped it wouldn't be in the confines of a hospital. A quick gunshot to the head or sudden snap of the neck would beat this, hands down.

Karl strode to the central desk and collected a zip lock bag containing his father's wallet, cell phone and a package of gum. He was given a white paper bag that held his father's clothing and shoes.

With a nod to the nurses, he made his way down the hall carefully avoiding peering into the rooms that held the dying. He chucked the white clothing bag into the trash container that stood outside near the smoker's area.

His nerves jangled at the key's metallic screech as it strained to turn the decaying lock. When he opened the door to the fourth floor walk-up, Karl was welcomed by stagnant, fetid air. Throwing open the window; he let the cool night air flood the room. Exhausted, he dropped the zip lock bag on the counter and lay down on his bed. Confused tears lined his face. Was he weeping for his father, his long dead mother or for himself?

CHAPTER 4

KARL WOKE CHILLED BY THE DRAFT FROM THE WINDOW. AS THE fog cleared from his mind, he knew by the way clanging garbage bins mixed with the steadily increasing hum of the early morning commuters that it was very early in the morning. Shucking off his shoes, he climbed fully dressed under the duvet. Too bloody early to get up, he thought. Sleep, however, did not return.

Abandoning his bed, he stood watching the city come alive. One by one his neighbours disappeared down the street to their no-name brand jobs that brought in a generic salary. A stab of jealousy pricked his soul. He had no such job and consequently, no salary. His money was steadily dribbling away. Unable to commit to a regular job, Karl picked up part time work and sometimes shady deals. Shrugging his shoulders, he brushed off his worries like a reptile shedding a layer of skin. There was always another coat underneath; always another opportunity around the corner.

As the coffee grew cold and the waitress impatient, Karl left a miserly tip and went to pay the bill. He was bored with his mundane existence and craved excitement. Just down the street, the Big B Casino beckoned. Blowing all but $30.00, Karl fed his cravings.

The next morning brought a swift reckoning. Karl paced his small apartment. The rent was due. He had very little food in the fridge and no beer. Throwing on his jacket, he skipped down the flights of stairs and out into the street. As he made his way to the casual laborers pick-up corner, he wondered if he would get lucky today. Lately, the jobs had been few and far between. Luck was with him.

"Need a week's worth of hard graft?" asked a balding, bearded contractor leaning out of a beater.

"Sure. What you got?"

"Tear down of the Quinten over on Maple Street. You know that old motel on the corner?"

"Yup. Works for me. What ya payin?"

"Min plus a dollar."

With a quick nod, Karl climbed in the back of the old Chevy and began his stop-gap job. Chuckling to himself, he'd had a brainwave. Sell the old man's property. It wasn't like he would ever want to live there again. He might even get a decent price.

◇◇◇◇◇◇

"Market's slow right now," warned Gary Champion, the realtor, as he took Karl's particulars.

Karl nodded trying not to look desperate. His plan had to work. Glancing at the balding realtor dressed in an expensive grey suit, he weighed his words carefully. "I need a pretty quick sale. Going to South America in the fall and need all the cash I can lay my hands on. What would it take for you to make this top priority…for you to bust your ass?"

Gary Champion smiled. "I always treat my clients well. I have the top sales in the area right now. A higher percentage in commission might encourage a little overtime now and then, but the market is in a downturn." Seeing his fish wiggle, the realtor added, "Isolated property on the coast is particularly difficult to shift."

Karl knew when he was up against it. "Okay let's say, four percent instead of three and a quarter if you can find a buyer before May 31. Three months should be lots of time for the top salesman in the area."

"Okay, what you got?"

Karl spread the deed, the will and the probate papers. Everything was in order. His father may not have appreciated banks, but he had kept meticulous records and all government papers. Harry had handed everything over to Karl before he passed. "You'll see all is in order. Probate papers came through last week. How much do you think the place will fetch?"

"What's your bottom line?" Gary asked.

"Whatever the market will bear. I don't want to give it away, but I need the cash as soon as possible. Besides, it's in both our interests, to get a good price."

Later that day the new posting, placed front and center in Southern Coast Realty's window, lured a very interested couple.

Live Off the Grid in West Coast Paradise
Lot# 2634 Pre-emption/Clear Title
160 acres of prime coastal real estate
The property consists of: a liveable cabin, several useable
out buildings, some cleared pasture, old orchard, timber
rights, oyster lease, dock, sizeable creek, beach, start of
a solar power system and some furniture and equipment.
Loads of extras.
Accessible only by water
3.25 hours from Rupert
Asking $185,000
Agent: Gary Champion
250 867 9121

Several faded photographs were arranged artfully across the bottom of the poster.

◇◇◇◇◇◇◇

Linking her arm in Sam's, Anna felt her spirits lift. They had just bought an 18 foot runabout. The sturdy cabin cruiser needed some minor cosmetic work, but the engine and all the mechanics had seemed fine. Now that they had made the decision to sell up and move, she could hardly contain her excitement. Smiling up at her husband, she chatted happily. "It's all coming together. We got that boat for a decent price. We've got lots left over for the land."

Sam wasn't listening. His attention had been taken by the ad in Southern Coast Realty. "Hey, this is new. We've got $185,000. Look at this…160 acres, buildings, pretty isolated by the sounds of it, and it's even got solar power stuff."

"It says it is a pre-emption. Isn't that one of those olden day deals where the government gave pioneers land and all they had to do was improve it in so many years?" Anna asked.

"No worries…it also says clear title." Sam's eyes shone as he studied the faded photos.

They scanned the poster intently. For $185,000 this property seemed almost too good to be true.

Opening Southern Coast Realty's door, Sam stepped inside and set the last piece of the puzzle in place.

Chapter 5

SARA YANKED THE HOOD FURTHER FORWARD TO COVER HER FORE-
head. Driving sleet was forcing its way past her loose headgear and
beginning to pool at the neck of her rain jacket. This might be good
rain gear, but only if you zipped up properly, she chided herself.

Over to her left, Mary huddled beside the wheelhouse sheltering
as best she could from the cold needle-like sting of the spring storm.
From the look of her sister's face, Sara knew Mary was starting
to withdraw into one of her silent times. The hunched shoulders
and closed face revealed the downward spiral that left Mary in her
impenetrable shell. Knowing the window was closing, Sara crossed
the heaving deck and sat down beside her troubled, younger sister.
"Crap weather, isn't it? Welcome to the West Coast," she joked as
she casually threw her arm around the waif. "Can only get better. I
think this is as cold as it gets on the coast. Dad said it might rain
quite a bit, but this is unusually cold for May."

Mary used her soaked sleeve to wipe salty spray and tears from
her face. "I sure hope so," she said through clenched lips. "My feet
are freezing in these rubber boots and my hands are too wet to ever
unwrinkle. I'll look like a prune the rest of the summer." Her weak
attempt at humour faded quickly as she reached over grabbing

Sara's arm. "Sara, what if this doesn't work? What if we lose all our savings, all the money from the house, everything?"

Sara pulled her coat tighter and leaned towards her sister. "Don't think like that," implored Sara, clasping her sister in a tight embrace. "This is not your fault. Everyone wants a new start, not just you. Mom and Dad hated the city life and me, well, I want an adventure."

"If only I could have been stronger and been able to stand up to Sharon and her gang, none of this would be happening. Every family has a weak link, and I'm it."

"Come on, buck up. Have you ever seen Dad so excited? This is his dream. All his life he has yearned to go back to the land and be self-sufficient. You know that. Now he can."

Silence mingled with the hiss of the wind and the spattering of the rain against the wheelhouse.

"You know, Sara," Mary continued. "I feel guilty that I'm so happy to have left my troubles behind. In the bush there will only be us. Will that be enough for you? Will you hate me after a while? You loved your friends, the pool and everything. Will you hate me for taking you away from all that?"

As wretched sobs erupted again from the miserable child, Sara fought against a rising tide of resentment. If she were honest with herself, she knew that she would miss her life in the city. Pushing down claws of doubt, she grabbed her sister's face, turning it towards her. "No more of this. I want to be here. I want to experience pioneer life. Mom and Dad want to test their skills and knowledge on this homestead. It's an adventure. I bet we would have done this even if you weren't being bullied. It was just a matter of time before Dad would have gotten fed up, anyway. You know Mom is always hankering after the freedom of her hippy childhood."

This brought a brief smile to Mary's face. Both girls had been amazed at their mother's immediate transformation into a free-spirited, long-skirted, boot-clad hippy chick as soon as she and Dad had made up their minds to leave the stifling city environment behind. Indeed, Anna, their mom, did make a good earth-child. Her face was wreathed in a constant smile replacing the guarded, tight lips that betrayed discomfort with urban life. She looked and acted years younger…more like an older sister than a working mom with responsibilities and worries that had etched lines into her cheeks and around her eyes.

Sara squeezed Mary's shoulders again. "Yes, she certainly looks happy these days, doesn't she? Come on; let's get inside out of this rain."

Mary pulled away. "No, no, I can't. Those fishermen stare at my face and besides its way too hot in there. You can't breathe. And I'm not going below deck in these waves. We'd be sick in minutes."

Sara had to agree. The seas were really rough with swells topping three meters. Every once in a while, they would feel waves crash against the bow. This sent showers of sea water over the forward deck. The stinging sleet stung any exposed skin.

She poked her head into the wheelhouse and asked how much longer it would take to reach their homestead.

"Maybe three, maybe four hours more. We get behind those islands soon and the wind will be less."

Spotting a discarded slicker behind the back bench, she glanced at the captain. "Can I borrow that for a while?"

He shrugged, "Sure, sure."

Rigging up a barrier to shield them from the driving rain, Sara made a cosy nest for Mary and herself. Together they snuggled down with their arms around each other. Two against the wilderness…two against the elements.

Sam and Anna needed no such protection. Leaning on the railing, they braved the oncoming wind and sleet much like they faced the world. The two of them, as one, could overcome most troubles. A little wind and rain was nothing.

Several hours later, the Korean boat rounded the point and headed into a narrow passage. Islands, fiords and forest became their new scenery. Once out of the wind, the boat slowed and chugged towards a distant point. As the conditions improved so did the spirits of the Lindholm family.

"Come up here with us," called Sam to his daughters. "Come and see where we are going." He held a chart in his hands. Pointing towards a small cabin overlooking the channel, he told them it was Thoresen Island. "Apparently that island belongs to the older brother…the one Karl told us about. He's the brother that left to set up another homestead after a falling out."

"Doesn't look like anyone's there," Anna commented. "I can't imagine living so isolated and all on you own."

"Boat's tied up at that dock," Sam said indicating a small dingy nestled in the cove. "Let's give a wave, anyway. He's our nearest neighbour and we may as well start off right."

As the Lindholms waved, their fish boat turned again and headed away from the forlorn island. The vessel motored on up the channel for a couple of miles with its weary passengers longing for this trip to be over. There was still some daylight left and they were anxious to unload their supplies from the fish boat and explore the piece of paradise they had bought.

The Korean captain slowed the vessel to a crawl and began to swing around the headland. Rough, craggy cliffs stood guarding the entrance to a small cove. As the boat neared a narrow weathered grey dock, the sun briefly peaked out from behind the scudding clouds. The rain eased and the wind became a mere wisp tossing the waves onto the sandy shore.

With spirits buoyed at the improving conditions, the small family smiled and cheered. The goats and chickens sensing their imminent freedom from their crates began to add to the chorus. The captain issued a few rough commands and the crew secured the fish boat to the worn posts jutting up from the dock.

"Too late now to unload everything and get back out to sea," the captain said gruffly. "Better to do it in the daylight anyway. Go ashore and look around. Sleep on board tonight."

"Yeah, you're right," agreed Sam. "Can't see the cabin, anyway. Wonder where it is? Christ, those animals are making a racket! We should at least unload them."

The captain laughed and nodded his head. "You sure you just got goats and chickens? Sounds like a whole damn zoo. Go find the cabin and we will see to the animals."

Two hours later, the family sat forlornly around the galley table. Their explorations of the homestead had revealed all was not as advertised. The 'liveable' cabin was inhabited by a packrat with all its accompanying stench and mess. Some of the outbuildings had roofs, but most were in a serious state of disrepair.

On the upside, there was a fast running creek with the best tasting water Sam had ever drunk and the remains of an old generator. Their brief foray into the surrounding land revealed a small meadow, a few ancient apple trees and what was once a garden plot.

"Well, we sure have our work cut out for us," Anna said resolutely. "Hey, it's nothing that we can't handle. Things will look better in the morning after a good night's sleep. Come on, let's eat up and get to bed. Captain Sun Soon-Chun will want to unload and get out of here early tomorrow."

Mary kept her eyes glued to her plate. Just as she feared, things were going from bad to worse. One of the goats had run off as soon as they had opened the crate. Now, it was wandering around in the bush at the mercy of whatever was lurking out there. The cabin stank and it looked like they had nowhere to live. Unconsciously, she began to rock. Sara gently put out her hand and touched Mary's knee. Dull eyes avoided hers, but the rocking ceased.

Sam gathered Anna into his arms. Lying quietly in the narrow bunk, they whispered assurances to each other.

The girls lay wide awake with only a musty futon between themselves and the grubby floor. Unable to resist, Sara started to scrabble her nails on the damp wood. Snickers and giggles erupted as Mary swatted her sister. "Cut it out, you twit. Cut it out." Mary was not afraid of mice but the memory of the smell from the cabin reminded her there were bigger rodents to be dealt with.

"Girls! Stop. It was nice enough of Captain Sun Soon-Chun to let us sleep in his quarters. Let's not keep him awake as well," admonished Anna. "Night, girls. Get some sleep. We have a hard day ahead of us tomorrow."

Captain Sun Soon-Chun stretched out on the padded bench in the wheelhouse. The members of his crew were strewn around the deck and in the forward bow. It was usual for them to sleep on deck, using the fore and aft bunks only in bad weather. Tonight it had cleared up nicely and most of the men were outside. As Sun Soon-Chun drifted off to sleep, he thought briefly about his passengers. They seemed eager and enthusiastic to start their new life, but he wondered if they were strong enough. He knew from Sam's reputation that he had many skills including carpentry, building, and book learning. His wife Anna had an air of confidence that came from a background of hard work and self-sufficiency. Poor girls, they were in for a shock, especially the youngest, the one with the birthmark. Her blank eyes and quiet demeanor hinted at serious trouble. Where was the spark that would help her weather the trials that were sure to come?

The next morning, Sara hurried along the path towards the first outbuilding. She had spotted the escapee standing in front of the broken door, trying to rejoin the herd. As she neared the shed, she slowed down and eased along quietly. "Oh there, you are," she cooed. "Not so nice on your lonesome, is it?" Hauling on the door, she stepped quickly inside to prevent the other three goats from escaping. Rattling the empty feed bucket, she tempted the orphan inside. "Silly boy, feel better now?" She left as quickly as she had entered. The goats would have to wait until everything had been brought ashore, for their next feeding. There was no time to waste as Sun Soon-Chun had made it plain they needed to get underway before the tide turned.

Quickly rigging the huge blue tarps between the closest outbuildings, Sam and his family valiantly helped the Koreans shift all the Lindholms' worldly possessions. Lumber, shingles and other building material soon vied for space with the farm equipment and solar panels.

"Why did we bring so much?" muttered Mary as she and Sara struggled to erect yet another tarp.

Sara grinned. "Maybe it's just as well we did bring all this stuff. This isn't at all what I thought it would be. Liveable cabin," she snorted derisively. "Mom's old army tent will be it for a while. How's Dad going to get the packrat out?"

She had to laugh as Mary put her first two fingers to her temple execution style. Mary surprised her every so often with her humour. She was glad that Mary's mood had improved. There was nothing like hard work to make you forget your troubles, however briefly.

"Girls, get a move on. Furniture is coming next and then the steamer trunks." Anna was standing off to one side of the rough gangplank with her hands on her hips. She reached up to blot the sweat that threatened to sting her eyes.

"Did you find the camp stove yet?" Anna asked on her next trip up the gangway. "I'll need you two to start some oatmeal for lunch. Can't have these men working and not feed them."

Slowly but surely the piles of provisions grew under the tarps. The Lindholms' small runabout was now securely tied to the other side of the dock and the fish boat looked less like a moving van.

Sam extended his hand towards the captain. As they shook, he looked earnestly at the man. "I can't thank you enough. If there is ever anything I can do to help you out, please don't hesitate to ask. Here's what I owe you," he said pressing an envelope of cash into Sun Soon-Chun's hands.

"Good to do business with you," declared the Korean. "We were going this way anyway and the cash is more than welcome. Fishing is not a sure thing." He turned and climbed aboard his vessel motioning to the deckhand to cast off.

As the boat drifted away from the dock, Sam could hear the engine as it tried to start. The engine's stuttering was soon drowned out by cursing and shouting from the crew. The boat slowly drifted further and further away.

Captain Sun Soon-Chun signaled Sam to get in his runabout and try to grab the towline. As he threw the heavy rope over to Sam he asked to be towed to the dock. "Don't know what's wrong," he yelled. "Dead, completely dead."

Sam and Shin Jong-Kyi, the first mate and engine man, worked long into the night. It was left to the women to set up the old tent and to cobble together some semblance of dinner. They fed and watered the goats and chickens; shutting them up once again in the ramshackle shed.

Around midnight, the weary men finished repairing the engine. They took it out into the dark bay for a preliminary test. Much to everyone's relief, the engine performed as it was supposed to.

"Good job," the Korean captain said as they neared the dock. "I thank you, Mr. Lindholm. I thank you."

As morning dawned, the grateful Koreans left promising to call in on their way back from the fishing grounds.

Finally, Sam and his family were left alone on their little patch of paradise. Not that they could see paradise through the sea of blue tarps. Anna simply shrugged and poured herself another cup of coffee from the already blackened pot.

CHAPTER 6

HIS $177,600, AFTER THE REAL ESTATE AGENT'S CUT, WAS NOT TOO bad for a piece of rock on the edge of the Pacific Ocean. Karl felt pretty pleased with himself. The real estate agent, Gary Champion, had called him last night with the final details.

Karl chuckled as he remembered meeting Sam and Anna Lindholm. Sam's eager eyes had literally shone with anticipation. Anna, the wife, couldn't keep her mouth shut with all her plans for a garden, goats and chickens. The kids had been quiet, especially the damaged one. What had that been on her face? Sure looked permanent, whatever it was. Poor kid must suffer a load of grief over that. He shrugged his shoulders at his brief moment of compassion. Life was tough and he had the scars to prove it.

He grinned as he fingered the cheque. The heavy bond felt good in his hand. Three blocks onwards, he entered the Bank of Nova Scotia and found his place in line.

"You certainly look happy."

Karl looked around and saw no one he recognized.

"Come into some good fortune?"

Unable to contain his excitement, Karl found himself in conversation with a total stranger, standing in line ahead of him.

The older gentleman reeked of cigarette smoke and possibly last night's festivities.

Grinning from ear to ear, Karl regaled his new-found friend with some of the more salient points of his amazing real estate deal. George, as the old duffer preferred to be called, listened intently.

"Sounds like you are one shrewd businessman," George complimented Karl.

Karl was intrigued. He often thought of himself as a man who could make a deal and this real estate transaction was proof of his abilities. This guy seemed to recognize talent when he saw it. "Yeah, I do well enough," he said as he pointed to the teller beckoning to George. "Think you're up."

It took quite a while for the banking to get done. Even after proving he had an account in that branch and their verifying the already certified cheque, he was told it would take several days to clear.

"How many is several?" complained Karl, standing impatiently in front of the small slip of a girl. "I need access to those funds."

"Like I said, a few days. The hold should be off by Thursday. It's drawn on a local bank, but it still has to go to Vancouver."

Karl glowered at the teller and loudly demanded to see her supervisor.

"No problem, sir," answered the girl. "But she will tell you the same thing. Just meet me at the customer service desk and we will get this sorted." She glanced apologetically at the long line of customers waiting for the only two tellers open, slid her closed sign over in front of her station and hurried over to customer service.

Karl noticed George standing off to one side of the long counter busily fiddling with some papers.

George looked up with a question in his eyes.

Karl shrugged and joined the teller and her supervisor.

"It's for your and our protection," stated the manager. "Bank policy clearly states that with cheques of this denomination, we must place a hold on the funds until it has gone through central clearing. There is nothing I can do. If you want I can return your cheque and you could try another bank, but I'm pretty certain most banks have the same policy."

Karl frowned. He only had an account in this branch. No other bank would cash a cheque this size for a non-customer. Those cheque cashing places took a huge percentage. Besides, he owed most of the ones in town for the payday loans he used when he ran out of casino money. "Damn," he swore softly. "Look, I'm flat broke. What can I withdraw? Surely, I can get a few bucks. The cheque is for one hundred and seventy-seven thousand."

"I can authorize two hundred. You've been a customer here since two thousand and one, but you did have trouble repaying the line of credit last year."

Karl shoved his cash in a pocket of his jeans as he strode out the door, nearly colliding with George in the foyer. "Sorry," he muttered. "Lousy fucking day."

"Whoa, sounds like someone needs a coffee. Better yet, let's grab a beer and some grub at that pub on the corner."

Karl quickly scrutinized the man. He seemed harmless enough and he had expressed quite an interest in his success. Yes, he could use some cheering up. Besides, he was starving. He hadn't had a bite to eat since last night. "Hey, why not. Need a drink after all that run around. They are holding my funds until the cheque clears in Van. Bloody regulations. Screw red tape."

On his third beer, Karl found George to be more than just an interesting old guy. Listening to stories of money made and money spent, he recognized a like-minded soul. It appeared that George knew everyone and had experienced a lot in his fifty-odd years on this earth. He had been a logger, a fisherman, a loan's officer and of all things an addiction councillor. Like Karl, he was orphaned and had few responsibilities.

"What are you planning to do with your new-found money? Going on a world tour? Paying off bills?" George asked innocently.

"No world tour for me. One hundred and seventy-seven thousand wouldn't cover the way I'd want to travel. Me, I like the luxuries…the finer things in life. You know wine, women and the slots."

George snickered, high-fiving Karl. "You're a man after my own heart. Spend it while you got it is my motto. Still, I've got a sure fired thing if you are interested."

"If it's so sure fired why aren't you rolling in it?" laughed Karl as he beckoned the waitress to bring another round.

"Just set it up, that's why. Best I keep it mum, though. I don't know you much and how do I know you won't go to the man?"

Karl carefully scanned the room. Lowering his voice, he quietly detailed the last legal scrape he had suffered.

"Easy enough to check on that," George said. "I got friends in high places. I got friends over at the court house."

"Go ahead. It's a matter of public information. I don't give a shit." Karl narrowed his eyes and glared at George. "Keep your deal to yourself if you want. I gotta visit the can."

By the time he got back, the older man was just closing his cell phone. Karl dragged the chair noisily across the greying wood floor. "Finished checking up on me?"

"Did better than that. I got you a line on a job."

"Don't want a stinking job. I got money coming next week. Time for a little R&R for this guy."

"Yeah, you'd like this job. Combines all your talents and will make you a shitload of cash. You need a stake though. You need to buy in. You could use some of that money you got coming in next week."

Karl stared at his drinking companion. "Told you, I don't need a job. I'll have money by next Thursday." He looked up in surprise as George McKinnon gave a snort. "What's so damn funny?"

"You're like me. Man…money just trickles away. There's never enough."

"Yeah"

"Hey, 177 thou's quite a bit, though. It'll last you a while."

"Maybe. But I got a bit of a problem with the slots and online poker. Would need to go hide out on some freaking desert island for it to last," Karl said slurping the dregs of his pint. "I'd best be off."

"Okay, see ya. Oh, here take my card in case you change your mind about the job. I can guarantee you double if not triple on your investment." George passed his gold embossed card over the table. He knew when to stop pushing and to let the deal settle.

Later in the week, Karl was at his usual haunt, the Big B Casino. Having finally received his money, he was looking to score some excitement. Standing by a bank of garishly lit slots, he slid twenty after twenty into the Fantasy Dragon slot machine— choosing his lines and bets, pushing the button until he ran out of chances. No rewarding bells or flashing winning lights erupted from the pole above this machine. Damn that was quick. His neighbour, a thin-faced senior with her hair pulled back in a scrunchie had won twice while he had been sitting there. It was not his night for slots, obviously.

Sauntering over to the entrance, he indicated to the security guard that he was going for cash. "Going for supplies Joe."

The Big B followed the provincial rules and located the nearest cash machine, outside the actual casino. It was over in a corner beside the bar. Karl crossed over to the ATM and slid his debit card into the machine. As he checked the receipt, he realized that he had spent over six hundred dollars in two days. Most of that had been laundered, here, at the casino.

The bar beckoned invitingly and Karl realized he hadn't eaten in quite a while. Slipping into a booth, he waited until the gum smacking waitress approached. "Just a Big B hamburger, fries and a Canadian, please."

"Be just a sec," she said with a weary smile, pausing to wipe the table with a grubby bar towel. "What kind of fries? Regular, wedges or curly?"

"Wedges, and hold the mayo on the Big B."

He looked at his receipt again. Christ, six hundred in two days. His luck was due to change. Perhaps he needed to up his game and try the Roulette or Black Jack tables. In September, he'd won big on Roulette in Vegas. Now, there was a great place for action. Lost in thought, he startled when the tired waitress slapped his meal down in front of him.

"Here you go. Want another Canadian?"

"Sure, may as well." Karl settled down to enjoy his burger.

"Well, hello there." A voice filtered into his drifting thoughts. "Spending some of that hard earned cash or should I say ill-gotten gain?"

George stood slightly off to one side of the booth with his stringy hair nudging his collar and his breath wafting a mixture of garlic and whiskey. Smiling, he held out his hand. "Remember me?"

"Of course. Sit down. Take a load off," replied Karl pleased to see his new acquaintance. "I was just grabbing a bite before I try to change my luck. Crapped out at the slots."

George pushed his girth into the seat opposite Karl. "I like Black Jack best but Roulette… treats me fine. More chance there, I think. Still you can lose or win big on both."

"After I finish this," Karl said through a mouthful of fries, "I'm gonna do some Roulette. Want to join me?" He wiped his lips with a wadded up napkin then threw it down covering the remainders of the cold meal. Draining his beer he nodded to George. "You coming or you got other pressing plans?"

George McKinnon shook his head. "In a bit. I've got a call to make and I'll have to get some cash at the machine. See you in there."

Both men went in opposite directions. Karl drifted over to the slots again to waste time until George returned.

Sliding one of those newer 'plastic' twenties between the hungry steel maws of Fantasy Dragon, he chose his lines and placed his bet. By the time George reappeared, he was grinning broadly. "Hey," he said as the older gentleman casually touched his shoulder. "Luck's changed. Let's hit the tables."

Spotting two vacant places, side by side at the second roulette table, Karl nodded to the dealer. "Empty?" he asked gesturing to the stools.

Sally, a blonde amazon of a woman, smiled. "Sure, place your bets, gentlemen. Place your bets."

George McKinnon, in spite of initially winning several spins, lost significantly. Feeling sorry for his companion, Karl suggested, "Let's try Jack for a while. More skill needed there. Perhaps your luck will improve."

Signalling to the passing waitress, George ordered two rum and cokes. Booze, here, was free and they were taking full advantage of this perk. The two men played on into the night, sometimes winning enough to keep it interesting, but more often losing. As the drinks worked their magic, the losses became a harsh reality.

"Crap," swore Karl as he came back from his third trip to the ATM. "I've spent a wad tonight. Down over fifty thou."

"The only way to recover is to bet the farm. Do the max," encouraged George slapping more money on the table.

The dealer winked at Karl and smiled.

"You brave like your pal here?" she asked.

He glanced at this comely blonde. Alcohol and the late hour overcame his last cautionary thought. "Sure, max me out."

One hand later, Karl and George McKinnon left the Big B totally tapped out.

"What the fuck am I going to do now? I've blown the entire lot except for the bit I put into those GICs the bank manager told me about. What in hell will I do now?"

"Sucks big time," agreed George. "I'm flying down to Vancouver the day after tomorrow. Gotta get back to camp."

He stopped behind the dumpster to relieve himself and then rejoined Karl who was standing dejectedly with hands shoved in his jean pockets, his head down, looking morosely at the sidewalk.

Seizing the opportunity, George roped his victim in. "Say, listen. You got any experience in the bush? There's this here logging outfit and they always want guys. Good money, three squares and bunk. They also fly you back to civilization every four weeks for one week R&R."

Karl looked at George with interest. "I need to get a decent job away from this God forsaken town. Think they'd hire me? I cleared brush when I was a teen, have my first year's mechanic's papers, been a camp cook. What do they need?"

"Well, I'm not sure, but if you aren't fussy I could get you hired on and then see what comes up. Want me to put in a word for you? Might be more than a job to be got, if you get my drift." said George as he stared at Karl. Here was a fit, strapping man with no family ties. He probably had a reasonable work ethic. One word from him and the boss would be more than willing. Besides, he rather enjoyed Karl's company.

"Hell, yes," Karl spluttered. "I want to blow off this place. Best stay away from the casinos for a while. I owe rent and don't have the cash to pay it. What do you mean by 'more than a job'?"

He listened carefully as George explained how he could put his considerable talents to use while working at a camp. This particular camp was rife with gambling and liquor. In the off hours, he could be guaranteed lots of Poker and Black Jack action. The only fly in the ointment, so to speak, was the cut management would take. Taking the briefest of moments to consider this opportunity and the predicament he was in, he grasped at the extended offer. "How much of a stake do I need?"

"What you got left? How quick can you cash in your GICs?" George asked.

"Tomorrow I can get to the bank. I'll have to pay a penalty, but what the hell. Not got much choice in the matter. How soon can you set up the deal?"

Grinning, the older man reached for his cell. Soon arrangements had been made. Both men were to come in on the same plane and Karl could start immediately. The camp cook had quit the day before and the boss's secretary was belly aching as she reluctantly filled in. Arranging his flight took just a few more moments.

Racing up the stairs to his fourth floor walk-up, Karl felt his heart beating faster. He loved change and it had been a long time since he'd had the chance to make some real money. Logging camps paid well. His cooking was rusty, but he knew how to make quantities of good home-style food. Besides, he could make himself useful after hours and maybe score a labour or mechanical job. Sure he only had completed one year of his mechanic's apprenticeship, but one engine was basically the same as another as far as he was concerned. He was a quick learner and followed orders well. He grinned. Life had definitely taken a turn for the better. Unwittingly, the brief thought that his father would have been proud, entered his mind.

As he breathed in stale air and old cigarette odours melding with the sour cabbage smell emanating from the apartment across the hall, he knew he wouldn't miss this clap trap. He had only minutes before the taxi; George had ordered for him, would be along to take him to the airport. His money had been easy enough to get, but he'd paid that hefty penalty for early withdrawal. Damn banks, always wanted their bit and more. Maybe his father and his uncle Sven had been right keeping most of their money in cash and easily accessible.

His head jerked up at the sound of the taxi's horn. Rushing to the window, he leaned out. "I'll be right down."

Karl threw his clothes into his suitcase and stuffed his work boots, hard hat and tools into a duffel bag. Three steps later, he was out the door and on his way down the hall. Nope, he wouldn't miss this dump at all. They could stick his deposit too. He was doing the midnight flit with no forwarding address. He was blowing this hole in the wall for good.

CHAPTER 7

THE GIRLS COULD HEAR THEIR FATHER CALLING. HIS VOICE carried on the slight ocean breeze as it mingled with the occasional screech of the seagulls and the soft lapping of the morning tide.

"Best we go see what he wants," Mary said reluctantly to her older sister. "Perhaps he needs more help with the pipes." She was referring to the system of pipes, catchment basins and ditches leading from the hillside creek to the large wooden cask near the cabin.

Her dad had been working on this ever since they had unloaded their stuff from the Korean fish boat earlier in the week. He was insisting the water system be the next thing to be completed. The trek up and down the steep hillside took too long. The heavy water-filled pails were cumbersome and more water got spilt than made it to the kitchen. Right now the creek was not running fast enough to spill over the rocks and onto the beach with any amount of flow. He was planning to reopen that channel once they were settled in. Eventually, water power was going to be used to supplement the solar power.

"Darn," muttered Sara. "I love it here on this beach." She glanced around absorbing the sights, sounds and smells clamoring for attention. "I never get tired of just being here. Look, I can see a way up that rock face." She pointed to a rough trail up the craggy boulders.

"I bet if we were careful, we could make it up there from the beach instead of going the long way around."

"Yeah, you're right. We could easily make it. Let's come back after lunch and check it out," Mary said as she turned obediently in the direction of her father's now impatient shouts.

"Where have you girls been? I've been hollering for a good ten minutes."

Mary stole a quick look at her dad. She hated it when he was cross. The knot in her stomach slowly released itself as she really looked at him. No, he wasn't angry with them…only wanting to get on with his task. "Sorry, Dad, we were down on that little sandy beach near the dock. I think there's a path through those rocks to the upper meadow. This afternoon Sara and I are going to try it."

"Well, just be careful, you little mountain goats. It's a long way to the nearest hospital and I'm not sure I want to deal with any broken limbs."

He shifted his attention to the flexible lengths of PVC pipe that lay scattered at his feet. "Girls, hand me the two longer ones after I climb up the bank." Sam grabbed the bucket packed with his tools, joiners, glue and clamps and scrabbled up the rocky cliff.

Mary squeezed her eyes shut as bits of debris and small rocks tumbled over the edge showering them as they waited patiently for Sam to get into position.

"Okay, hand me the pipe."

Sara inched her way halfway up the cliff to just below her dad. Hanging onto a root, she planted her feet firmly and then reached down with her free hand. Mary slid the wavering pipe up to her sister sending another shower of dust over herself.

With her legs beginning to tire from her uncomfortable perch, Sara switched back and forth from one leg to the other.

Eventually, Sam coupled the new pipe and asked for the second.

She passed up that one and then eased her way back down to her waiting sister. "Should be long enough, hey Dad?"

Sam nodded. "Both of you can go help your mom, but make sure you're listening for me. I might need you on the next section."

The girls sauntered over to the cabin well aware of the scrubbing and sweeping that was in store for them.

"Cheer up," joked Sara. "At least we're not doing Algebra."

"Yes. I don't miss that classroom one bit. Nice that homeschool doesn't start until the fall, isn't it? I don't mind the hard physical stuff we have to do here; near as much as trying to concentrate on Mr. Vance's long winded explanations." She grabbed a stiff straw broom which was propped up against the far wall and began tackling the last of the dirt and leaves that still littered the cabin floor.

Sara started towards the steep path that led to the creek, carrying a large plastic water bucket. "Hope Dad gets that system in quick. This hauling water is getting very old." With a wave, Sara was off into the sunshine leaving Mary sneezing in the dim recesses of the old cabin.

◇◇◇◇◇◇

Anna glanced up as Sam and the girls entered the old army tent that served as their kitchen and eating area. They were covered in dust and grime. "Do wash up before you sit down," Anna ordered. "This may be the middle of nowhere, but we do have standards," she teased, shaking her head at her rag-tag family.

"Did," Sam grinned and held out two clean palms shining whitely in contrast to his dirt encrusted arms. "No point in doing more. I'm just going to get covered again. On the last of it, though. By tonight we should have water running into the barrel in the garden."

Anna crossed over to him, slipping into his arms. Tilting her head upwards, she gazed into his soft brown eyes. "Okay then… since you're promising water by tonight." Sam patted her bottom and sank gratefully into the camp chair beside the planks that made up their makeshift table. He reached for the pitcher of water and poured for all of them. The cool liquid snaked down their throats erasing the heat and the dust of their labours.

As her hungry crew tucked into last night's leftover stew, Anna frowned to herself. Already the vegetables they had brought with them were wilting and some were almost inedible. She needed to get started on the cold storage as soon as possible. She had noticed a small cave in the slope of the rocky hill that lead to the upper meadow.

"Can you check out that cave I was telling you about?" she asked Sam. "We need to find somewhere to store the veg and goat milk before long. It's quite warm today and stuff is starting to go. And there's no point in having the potatoes and root vegies getting soft as well. I can pick some wild greens for salads but it will be a while before that garden can be planted. Then who knows how long before we get anything from it?"

"The girls can look at it before they head down to the beach this afternoon," he said. "Just mind yourselves, girls. Chuck a couple of rocks in first, in case of critters."

Mary shot a worried look at her father. "What kind of 'critter' are we talking about?"

Sam chuckled.

As her pallor faded to a chalky-grey, Mary reached out a trembling hand towards Sara. Her eyes cast down and she repeated herself, faintly. "What kind of a critter?"

Instantly regretful, Sam tried to make light of Mary's sudden spiral. "Oh, I don't know…maybe the cousin of our friendly packrat or a family of skunks. Don't you worry. Pitch in a couple of rocks and sing loudly. Nothing will make them run quicker than your sister's singing." It was a standing joke that Sara was musically challenged. This usually brought a smile to Mary's face, but not this time.

Anna hastened to reassure her youngest. "Dad's only teasing you, Mary. That cave isn't big enough to be home to anything that could hurt you. I think it only goes in a couple of feet. But it should be much cooler in there than outside. It will keep the food cold. We'll have to put everything in those yellow pails with lids or we will be feeding mice." She passed the bannock around again. Giving Sam 'the look', she hugged her daughter. "Tell you what, let's all go explore the cave and we might even have time for a swim in that shallow pool by the rocks. I'm dying for a good clean up."

Damn, she could smack Sam up the side of the head sometimes. He wasn't the one who had to comfort Mary when she woke trembling from whatever memories ruined her sleep. Holding her frightened child in the darkness, she often fought back tears of helplessness as she realized the extent of cruelty and damage those dreadful bullies had inflicted. It did, however, seem like Mary was making some improvements as the nightmares were coming less frequently. She sometimes caught glimpses of the old Mary as she watched her daughter tramping the beaches and sitting in the ebbing light after a day's work.

This was a good move, for the whole family. They were growing stronger and more resilient. Sam's face was peaceful as the cares of the city were gradually slipping away, erased by the physical toil that had become his days. Hard work was definitely a catalyst for change. It had only been a couple of weeks, but even their bodies were changing with their soft pudgy flesh morphing into hardening muscle and cheeks radiating sunshine and wind. She, herself, was sleeping better even if it was in a sleeping bag on the hard ground in the second tent. If they continued to making their excellent progress, they would be in beds in the cabin soon. Sam wanted the water system finished first and then he was going to start on the garden. It had to be dug and turned over before they could even start to think about planting. They had to get the seeds in the soil soon if they were going to have enough time to mature the crops. There was always something. "Are you coming too?" she asked Sam.

"No, I'd best finish with the pipe before we lose the afternoon sun. I'd really like to be done. You go with the girls. The three of you ladies would scare off any skunks skulking around." Sam smiled as he picked up his hat, shoved it over his wiry curls and set off through the tent flap.

◇◇◇◇◇◇

Half an hour later, the trio were closing in on the cave entrance. To the casual observer, there was nothing unusual about this section of the cliff. The low, narrow hole was concealed by several large evergreen bushes. You had to travel past the bushes and look back before you could see the mouth of the cave. Hidden from the elements, it was a perfect place for a larder. You couldn't ask for a better location. It was an easy five minute walk from the cabin.

"Here it is, girls," called Anna as she spied the opening. "I nearly missed it."

Mary suddenly hung back. Memories of the dank stairwell smelling of mould and urine flooded her mind.

Sara sensed her fear and stopped. Holding her sister's hand firmly, she whispered. "There is nothing to be scared of. No one can get you here. We're safe. We are miles away from Sharon. We have mom with us. We're safe, we're safe."

Anna got to her knees and squeezed under the shallow lip of the overhanging rock.

Sara and Mary slid in after her. Sara's mantra echoed in Mary's ears. "We're safe, we're safe."

As Mary felt welcome coolness and smelt damp earth, peace stole over her like a soft blanket. Wrapping herself in comfort, she breathed deeply and let her mind relax. For the first time since the incident with Sharon's gang, she felt totally secure. It was a wonderful feeling. Nothing was going to hurt her here. Nothing.

The cave opened up into a small, low-ceilinged room. Once their eyes grew accustomed to the dim light, they could see several ledges that would be good for holding the food buckets. An old wooden crate lay on its side and an antique oil lamp hung from a peg driven into the rock wall. It seemed as though the previous owner had also used this cave for storage.

Anna sniffed the air. "No stink of packrats, and definitely no skunks around here," she said. "I think we've found our fridge, root cellar and hidey hole all in one."

Crossing over to the lamp, she lifted it and shook it. No liquid remained, but the mantle and wick seemed to be intact. "We'll have to bring some oil up here and see if it works. Sure would be nice to have a little more light in here."

More detailed searching revealed an old jar of some kind of preserves, a box of strike anywhere matches, and a discarded pocket knife.

"Oh look, Mom," said Sara as she held out some kind of a nest. "I wonder what made this." Passing it over to her mom, she dusted off her hands on the sides of her pants.

"Could be a mouse or maybe some kind of owl…Dad will know. Let's bring it back with us," Anna suggested.

With that the explorers crouched down and crawled out of the cave. They stood silently, blinking in the sudden sunlight. The view from the entrance was magnificent. Waves bounced off the dock and the rocks that lined their small beach. Far out to sea, the endless horizon glinted with varying shades of blues and greens.

"Oh, it's so beautiful here," breathed Sara. "I'm so glad this is our home now." She reached over and drew her sister into a friendly embrace. "You glad we came?" she asked.

A cloud of worry skittered over Mary's face, but she smiled bravely. "Of course, I just hope it works out for everyone. I couldn't bear it if this whole adventure turns out badly. What if you want to go to university? What if we don't have enough money to live in this paradise? You know there are things we will have to buy. Dad is already running out of lumber. It is taking so much to repair the old cabin. And what if someone gets dreadfully sick…you know the dying kind of sick?"

"Oh, give over," Sara chastised her sister. "Give Mom and Dad some credit, will you? They thought of all those things and more. You don't think we would have come if they weren't a hundred percent sure. We all did a lot of planning. Think of all those first aid courses. I know they have money in mutual funds and the bank. We didn't spend it all getting here. Grandma wouldn't have let them be that stupid."

Listening to her oldest daughter calm her sister, Anna had to admire her. Sara knew how to deal with Mary's fears— with no nonsense, hard, cold facts. Over the top of Mary's head, she winked at Sara. "Come on, worry wart. Let's go practice those swimming lessons. Grandma would have my life if she knew how timid you were in the sea. Really, it isn't that much different than swimming in the city pool with a dozen kids flailing around and kicking up a storm. Waves are waves. It's a darn sight cleaner too."

With that they meandered down to the beach collecting a couple of big beach towels on the way. Shouts and screams erupted as they raced into the cold sea.

CHAPTER 8

KARL LOOKED AROUND AT THE CROWD GATHERED IN THE MUNICI-pal airport. George was nowhere to be seen in this mob of workers waiting to fly out to bush camps. Everyone seemed to know everyone else and the volume rose as more and more men came to stand in line to check their baggage. With his suitcase in hand, he joined the shortest line kicking his heavy duffel along as the line crept towards the counter. "Hey…Susie," he said as the friendly agent greeted him with a lipsticked smile. "How's it going today?"

Her eyes arched in surprise at her name, but then she quickly relaxed as she realized he had simply read her name tag. "Fine. Do you have your reservation number handy?"

Within minutes, he was through security and waiting in the departure lounge for flight 906, the first leg of his journey to the middle of nowhere. Away from the turmoil and noise of the main terminal building, he began to lighten up a bit. Still, where in hell was this George guy? Last night, it had seemed like a good idea to take this job, but he knew very little about it. He needed George to run interference and to smooth out any wrinkles. Relief flooded over him as he saw a familiar figure striding into the room with his boarding pass in hand.

"Sorry, sorry," gasped George as if he'd just finished a five kilometer run. "Bloody taxi was late. Any trouble checking in?"

"No. I had the reservation number and lots of ID. No trouble at all. Some wicked crowd out there."

George McKinnon nodded. "Yup, sure is. We get into Vancouver at ten-thirty. Grab a quick transfer to the Sky Wind terminal downtown in the harbour and then hop a Beaver to take us into camp. Usually the crummy takes the guys in, but we're in luck; Fred is making an extra flight with the new computer hardware. Can't have that stuff bouncing over logging roads. Love those Beavers. Land just about anywhere."

As he listened to George rhapsodize on and on about the stellar qualities of one of the favorite bush planes of the interior, Karl's heart sank. He detested small planes and particularly hated landing on water. Damn, he'd thought it would at least be a Cessna. Those beat the crap out of f'ing Beavers, any day. Beavers were as old as the ark and he'd read about that crash in the interior just last week. Damn.

Karl tried to relax on the two hour leg to Vancouver, but by the time he landed, he was badly in need of a drink. "What time does that Beaver take off?" he asked his companion casually. "We got time for a bite?"

"Sure, but let's wait until we get downtown. There's this restaurant bar that serves the best burgers around. Licensed too. I could do with a couple of brews."

The taxi let them off across from Harbour Air. After walking for a couple of minutes, they reached a hole-in-the-wall café. "You sure this is the place?" queried Karl as they entered a smoke filled, dingy room.

"Yup. Been here lots. Here's where the bush cowboys eat. Best burgers this side of Whitehorse. It's a real look into the world of the bush pilots. I come here as often as I can when I'm flying into camp."

As they took the only available table, Karl signalled the waitress. "We're in a bit of a hurry. I can make it worth your while if you can get our order in fast. I'd like two beers and your burger special. My friend here…" He glanced at George expectantly. "What will you have? My treat."

He watched George nod and hold up two fingers, indicating he'd have the same as Karl had ordered.

As Karl downed one of the beers quickly, he caught George checking him out. Anxious not to appear nervous, he slowed down on the second beer. "Thirsty. Must have been all the salt in those in-flight snacks," he said.

Karl took in the scene. Over at the bar stood several men laughing and joking with a grizzled character that seemed straight out of the movies. The older man wore baggy blue jeans and a moth-eaten grey woollen sweater. The greasy ball cap, covering his long hair, skimmed his bushy brows and allowed just a peek of the man's startling blue eyes. A roguish, reddish-grey beard completed the picture. 'Grizzly Adams' had quite a following. The men were hanging on his every word. The man never had an empty glass.

George McKinnon laughed as he noticed where Karl's attention was focused. "Colourful old bugger, eh? One of the older bush pilots. Believe he's from Anchorage, originally. Now flies for anyone that'll hire. Word has it he has a bit of a booze problem."

As they sat munching their burgers and fries, they listened in on the conversations drifting from the bar. It appeared that 'Grizzly Adams' had been everywhere and done everything. The more he drank the better the stories of crashes, near misses and raw adventure became.

Karl's dread increased enormously. By the time they were finished eating, he was ready to chuck it all in. Just one problem, there was no way out. He was hooped. The crummy had left hours ago and they were due at the camp this afternoon.

George asked for the bill. "Well, we'd best be going. Fred told us to meet him by three o'clock. The light gets a little tricky the further you go into the interior mountains. Need to be at camp by six at the latest."

Karl threw a couple of twenties on the table.

He made a dash to the can just before take-off. The beers had worked their way to his nervous bladder. Hell, he'd been on these pieces of shit before. This was nothing. He could do it... had to.

"Welcome aboard. Hop right into that front seat beside me," said Fred, their pilot for this flight. "George has been on this flight so many times; it's old hat to him. He can snooze in the back."

Karl nodded. "My first time in one of these. You fly these puppies much?"

Fred laughed. "No worries. I've been flying Beavers most of my life. You're in good hands."

With the door still open, the pilot manipulated the controls on the dash; starting the sequence for takeoff.

The pilot coaxed the reluctant engine. The machine began tick-tick- splutter-coughing into rhythm. Puffs of blue, shot from the exhaust, permeated the cabin with a sickening stench. He leaned out, closed the door and began cutting through the waves towards the pass.

Karl's hand tightened reflexively on the edge of his seat as Fred eased the control column back towards his lap and pushed open the throttle.

The plane picked up speed. As spray rose from the edges of the floats, the skies opened up. Rain sheeted the windscreen. Fred peered myopically through the window.

Karl closed his eyes willing the shuddering machine up into the air. The floats skittered over the white caps. He felt the Beaver lift and lurch vibrating as it rose into the sky. Then the whole plane rattled as Fred banked to the right.

Karl grabbed at the edge of his seat again as his whole body slid towards the ocean. His eyes widening in terror, as he pictured himself skidding off his perch and tumbling into the sea. Held in by an impossibly narrow seat belt, he clenched his butt cheeks trying to find purchase on the slippery leather seat. Instinctively, he let out a yelp as vertigo took over forcing him to close his eyes against the vision of his impending doom.

Gradually, the plane levelled. The flight smoothed out and the steady drone of the engine filled the tight space. He let out his breath and caught a slight smile as it stole across George McKinnon's face. *Asshole.*

Fred nonchalantly reached into the lunch bucket between his and Karl's seat. Fishing out a huge sandwich, he offered Karl a bite.

"Hate these things. I like complete control over everything — machines, women, and Lady Luck," Karl muttered, turning to stare out of the rain-covered window. He was appalled at the sight of oil dribbling along the bottom of the windshield. He traced the dribble to the cowling. *Engines need oil…engines seize up and stop if they run out of oil.*

"Hey, is that normal?" he shouted pumping his fist towards the black streaks.

Fred didn't hear over the engine noise.

Karl tapped the pilot on the shoulder and pointed to the leaking oil. Fred, a seasoned bush pilot, swept his eyes to where Karl was indicating and then simply gave the thumbs-up sign.

For the rest of the trip, Karl kept compulsively checking to see if the stream of oil had increased. Smells radiating from Fred's half-eaten salami sandwich, turbulence, fear and what beer was left in his gut, churned. He retched and reached for his airsick bag, but it was too late. The odour from the vomit on the floor filled the cabin. Soon he was emptying his stomach, filling both his and George's airsick bags.

Turbulence increased as they skirted a thunderstorm just west of the Coastal range. Updrafts tossed the Beaver around like driftwood on swells. The engine thrummed steadily as the workhorse of the North carried on. Occasionally, lightning punctuated the air followed by a loud clap of thunder. Rain continued to pelt the windshield.

Karl hoped that Fred could see out the window better than he could. He fought the claustrophobic feeling bearing down on him. Breathing through his mouth, he attempted to quell his rising panic.

Just as suddenly as the rain had started, the skies cleared and the men could see for miles. Descending to just over five hundred feet, Fred cruised over the tallest treetops. Lakes lay scattered like broken mirrors ruffled in coarse greenery. Scraggly mountains peppered the landscape and were in turn reflected in the watery kaleidoscope. Sunshine bounced filling the cabin with light.

As they approached a long narrow lake, Karl could see several fishing boats leaving long curved wakes as they trolled. The pilot made a low circuit over the lake, checking for deadheads and rocks. One by one small crafts headed to the shoreline to wait out the landing.

Karl looked at the water, horrified. Blood thundered in his ears as he realized just how narrow and shallow that lake was. The frigging boats were in the way. He paled as he remembered the vivid account of the crash in this lake several years ago. Grizz had obviously embellished the story, but it had happened. Who's to say history wouldn't repeat itself, today?

Fred shouted over his shoulder, "Okay, hang on to your Saint Christopher, we're going to give it a go."

He levelled out the turn and approached the head of the lake. Throttling the engine back, he angled the floats towards their destination. Just before touchdown, Fred aborted; rising once again into the blue sky. "Gotta go round. Sorry about that. One of those frigging boats started to cross the bay. Stupid bugger. I'll try again. If he pulls that again, he'll be sushi."

Karl's fingers gripped the seat with fear-fueled strength. Offering up an atheist's prayer, he hung on for dear life.

With a slight chatter of water under the floats, the pilot settled the Beaver on the calm surface of the lake and taxied to the dock.

As he disembarked, Karl stepped in the vomit. Discreetly he walked along the edge of the lake, rinsing off his boots. He could see what must be the foreman coming down the trail towards the dock. *Bloody hell*, he thought to himself…*great first impression.*

The foreman grinned as he held out his hand to Karl. "Was it a good trip… except for the landing? Pretty hard to get used to Fred's driving," he joked, slapping Fred on the back. "Hey, man, how's it going? That old lady of yours still giving you grief? Any time you wanna trade her in give me first dibs. She's a looker, your missus."

He gave George a cursory nod. "This here's your new guy?"

George made the introductions. "Ralph, Karl. What Ralph says goes. He reports directly to Manfore Corp and he's the boss here at camp. By the same token, if you want for something he's your man to go to," explained George emphatically.

"Welcome aboard, Karl. Best we get you signed up and give you your keys to the bunkhouse. Leave that stuff here," he said pointing to Karl's suitcase and duffel. "Joe can bring them up when he brings the rest of the cargo."

After a bit of chit chat, the men strode quickly up the trail leading towards a scraggly row of Attco trailers. Arranged in two rows, the metal clad trailers resembled a parked train without cheerful graffiti. Small windows were open to the cooling evening air and one or two doors were propped open revealing untidy interiors. Men at camp were no tidier than when they were at home; probably less so as they didn't have naggers to help them along. Karl shook his head slightly. He enjoyed a tidy atmosphere and if the rooms were any indication, this camp might be a dump.

The main office wasn't much better. Every available surface held a tower of papers and several computer screens glowed wearily. Ralph waved his arm dismissively. "The place is a tip. Marilyn won't clean and cook. She only does one or the other. Since Herbie quit last week, she's been doing double duty and bitching like crazy. You'll start out in the kitchen until we hire the next bull cook. Money's the same as most camps, but we are a land of opportunity…if you get my drift."

Karl stole a look towards George.

"You did fill him in, didn't you?" Ralph asked George. "He knows why he's here, doesn't he? You said he had talent."

"Sure, sure. He knows what's up," assured George with a warning nod to Karl.

Karl said nothing and nodded his head as if he understood what was expected.

"Okay, then. Here are your bunkhouse and room keys and this here silver one is the key to your strongbox. Unload your gear. I'll go chase up Marilyn and see what's delaying supper." With a nod to the two men, Ralph strode out of the office and over to the center trailer.

In the confines of his small room, George and Karl discussed what was in store for Karl at camp. Yes, he would be cooking, but his real job was to fleece the workers. Karl would be running Poker and Black Jack. Apparently, George had done a great job selling Ralph on his gaming skills.

"Best you live up to your rep," warned George. "Ralph and I go a long way back and we got a good thing going here. The men get first rate entertainment and we make a bundle. So long as the big guys at Manfore get their cut, we're free to rake it in. Don't fuck it up."

Karl did his best to hide his surprise. Bravado kicked in and suddenly he was on board for the ride. Hell, sure he was good at the tables and poker. It was easy to fleece as long as the marks didn't catch on to his ways. "You ain't seen the half of my considerable talent," boasted Karl. "Casinos in town have too much security. It's hard to scam those buggers, but who here is keeping house? Between the two of us, we can make a fortune. Sure is crap for a room though."

They stood looking around the nine by nine space that passed for a bedroom. A single bed stretched along one wall with a desk, chair and storage drawers occupying most of the remaining area. Beside the desk was a small bar fridge with a microwave oven perched on top.

"What's through here?" asked Karl, opening a door beside the bed. He stepped into the filthiest bathroom he'd ever seen. The toilet was almost overflowing; paper towels crawled out of the excuse for a waste basket and the tub looked as though it had never seen a maid. A one cup coffee pot clung desperately to the edge of a cracked sink. A sour smell of shit and vomit permeated the tiny enclosed space.

"You have to keep you own rooms clean at this camp," George mentioned, casually. "You share the can. I guess your neighbour doesn't care much for housekeeping. Johnson had your room last." He reached over and flushed the toilet. "Hey, at least it works.

Cleaners and stuff are in that cupboard you saw by the trailer entrance. Marilyn will change the sheets once a week, but that's about it."

Karl shrugged.

"I'll leave you to it. Dinner is ready when you hear the gong. I'm going to get my stuff squared away then and go for a beer." George left Karl to himself.

Karl sauntered down the narrow hallway and retrieved some cleaning equipment. After he tackled the grungy bathroom, he swiftly changed the bedding and swept the floor. The room was passable, but just. He wasn't that fussy, still he wasn't going to live in those conditions. He'd make damn sure his neighbour did his share of the bathroom chores, if he knew what was good for him.

Marilyn was overjoyed to discover Karl was her replacement. The big bosomed gal took to him as soon as she laid eyes on him.

Handsome and charming when he wanted to be, Karl had her eating out of his hand. "Not sure what to do here, Marilyn," he said smoothly. "This is my first camp gig. I have cooked for groups, but not in a bush camp."

"No worries. It's simple enough for anyone who has cooked for large crowds before. The guys aren't too fussy. Just don't get fancy. I'll show you the ropes."

Soon she was showing him the equipment and where everything was stored in the industrial kitchen. She helped him prep for breakfast the next day. After a little instruction on the temperamental cook stove, quantities to prepare and the likes and dislikes of the men, Karl was given free rein.

Marilyn disappeared back to her old job of cleaning and office work; only checked on him occasionally. While he wasn't much of a pastry chef, Karl was quite popular for his hearty, everyday specials. The men looked forward to his meals at the end of their long workday.

Towards the end of the week, Karl was also introduced to the second and more important part of why he was hired. Gradually, George let it be known that Karl could play and had been quite successful at the casinos on the coast. Never ones to let a newcomer steal the glory, the workers vied eagerly to be invited to play. These games were held in a small trailer set some distance from the main camp. Poker and Black Jack were the star attractions with lots of beer and pot to up the ante.

Trudging back to his bunkhouse after a late session, Karl complained to George. "Christ I'm bushed. Gotta do breakfast in three hours."

"Yeah…would feel better if we were making a bundle but we aren't," agreed George, slyly. "This bunch is pretty good at Poker and excellent at Black Jack. Got any ideas how we can turn this around? Shift changes in two weeks and the guys start hanging on to their money when it gets towards home time."

Karl laughed. "Sure, but you might not want to hear it. We could fix the games. Would there be any flak from the big guys if we did?"

"Hell, no. All they care about is their cut. Sometimes, I think they'd prefer just running tables to operating a logging outfit. Besides, we don't have to let on. You got a way?"

"Yeah, I'm beat though. Fill you in after breakfast is over. In fact, I'll demo on you. That way you can see how foolproof it is." He slammed through the common door to the bunkhouse and turned into his room. Not bothering to do more than take off his shoes, Karl sank down on his bed. Three hours came and went as quick as quick.

As he stirred the golden liquid in the three cast iron frying pans, he rehearsed his moves. The eggs caught in one of the pans making him swear. With a quick swish of his wooden spatula, he lifted the hardening mess straight into the serving tray. Slopping the contents of the other pans on top of the first batch, he mixed everything together concealing the overcooked portion. A few unnecessary sprigs of parsley and no one would be any the wiser. Texas toast and bacon completed the meal.

"Morning, guys. Come and get it," he called to the men who had arrived earlier and were sipping the strong mud that passed as coffee. The guys shuffled over and began loading their plates.

"You up for a game tonight?" he asked Earl as he paused in front of the cooling scrambled eggs.

"Nah, gotta hold on to the bucks now. No point in even going home if I got nothing to show for it. Last time I did that, she told me to bugger off. Took a whole lot of sweet talking to get round that one."

"How 'bout you, Tim…up for it? Or are you pussy whipped as well?"

Tim sneered. "No, got no woman waiting for me. I'm footloose and fancy free you might say. Just got to pay the alimony and the rest is mine. Who else is playing?"

"Don't know. Have to get at least four to make it worthwhile. Figure it will be poker tonight."

Several of the crew indicated they'd play. George came over to the serving area as the last of the men slammed out through the screen door. Trucks started to rev up and soon the camp was left in relative quiet.

"Well, got enough marks for tonight?" George grinned and slapped Karl's shoulder. "When will you be done here?"

"Gotta prep chili for lunch and set the loaves to rise. Figure I got half-hour to spare around ten-thirty."

"Okay, see you then."

Karl opened his strong box and took out his doctored decks. These cards had almost put him in the poorhouse, but they were worth every penny. The cards and his special infrared contact lenses made for a winning combination. Sure, there were people who doubted it was possible, but you get what you pay for. He'd found them online on a Romanian website. The five decks of marked cards and three pairs of the lenses had cost him over four grand.

Smiling to himself, he removed a set of lenses and a deck of cards. He closed the box and stuck it back in the closet. If all went well, there would be more in there than decks and contacts. He'd been quite successful in Montana and here in a dimly lit trailer it would be even easier to score. No one would suspect a thing. These rubes were pretty unsophisticated. He already wore contacts during the day and these babies matched his eye colour and were thin, real thin. To the casual observer, they were virtually impossible to detect.

After covering the drain in the bathroom sink with a layer of paper towel, Karl opened the contact lens case. Usually he wasn't so careful; however these contacts had cost a fortune. Spritzing a lens with solution, he rinsed it carefully. Opening his mouth to steady his eye movement, he quickly deposited the lens on his iris. Blinking twice, he rotated the lens slightly to ease out a tiny air pocket. After repeating this practiced procedure, he was all set. Now he'd show George his solution to their cash flow problems.

George McKinnon knocked on the door and entered without waiting for an invite. It was past ten forty-five and Karl would have to be back in the kitchen by twelve. Lunch was usually served from one until two.

Karl was sitting at his desk, shuffling cards. "Pull up that chair," he said motioning to the battered stool in the corner.

George watched carefully as they played. There was no sleight of hand or visible movements that would indicate an improper deal. Often, Karl won, but so did George. It seemed that Karl was just luckier.

"Okay, I give up. What's the deal? How are you doing it?"

Karl smiled. "High tech stuff. You ever heard of infrared?"

"Sure, but that stuff only works in the movies."

"Don't be too sure…look." Karl then dealt a hand and then read each card that George was holding.

George McKinnon was blown away. He stared at Karl. He examined the cards. He couldn't see any markings. Karl dealt another hand.

"Son of a bitch, it does work. Son of a bitch. Come here," he demanded. "Let's see those eyes of yours. Yeah, I can see the contact, but it's really hard to tell. Can you wear your glasses as well or are these prescription lenses? Your glasses would hide them big time."

"Plan to. The guys are used to seeing me in glasses, especially when I play cards. No one will clue in. Particularly if I let them win some hands and don't wipe the floor with them. Done this before in Montana. They're too sharp in Vegas. Be real easy here. It isn't exactly Caesar's Palace!"

The two men planned their strategy. George was to lose tonight. He'd be really frustrated and demand a rematch the following evening. A couple of nights like that and the trap would be set. Pay day wasn't until Friday and it gave them six days to recoup their 'losses' and more. By the time the shift changed again, the crew would be up for some more of the same. Entertainment was scarce around camp especially after dark. There was no satellite TV and the internet was sporadic. Most of the men played video games, but even that got tiresome. Besides, gambling got in your blood. Lady Luck had to be on your side eventually.

Karl looked at his watch and swore quietly. "Bloody hell, gotta run or I won't have the bread done and cooled enough for cutting." He grabbed the cards and shoved them into the strongbox again. With no time to remove the lenses, he simply put on his glasses and disappeared out the door. "Slam the door shut would you? I have my keys."

CHAPTER 9

LISTENING TO THE RAIN LASH AT THE PLASTIC COVERING THE window openings and to the wind howling as it pummelled the homestead perched on the headland, Sara was thankful to be in the cabin at last. They had moved most of their household goods, furniture and bedding in the day before.

She reached her hand out and rubbed Mary's shoulder. Their narrow beds were so close that it was hard to squish between them, but the girls didn't mind at all. Mary was still waking with night terrors and Sara could often comfort her by simple touch. Mary, lost in the dreams, no longer lashed out with her fists. She had moved on to cowering and shielding her head. As she grew used to Sara's gentle touch, she would slowly uncurl and begin sobbing quietly. Anna was now leaving that task of settling Mary to Sara.

Since those senseless attacks, Mary seemed to relate better to Sara, anyway. Was it because they were closer in age? Perhaps Mary could sense her mother's helplessness. Sara accepted her and thought only to comfort. Anna needed to fix things and could not.

"Hey, you still awake?" Sara whispered softly.

Mary turned and pushed herself up on her elbow. "As if anyone could get to sleep in this storm. Thank God we finished the cabin before it set in. Not sure the tent would still be upright."

"Yes, it sure is nice to be warm and dry. Can't believe this weather in May, can you? Dad did say there would be a few storms, but somehow I was expecting it to be more in the winter."

◇◇◇◇◇◇

"Girls...go to sleep in there." Anna's voice rose above the howling wind. "If this weather clears up, we have planting to do tomorrow. I don't need you to be complaining that you're tired." She was anxiously waiting for them to drift off. The curtain between Sam, herself and the girls was pretty darn thin. They were counting on the wind to mask any noises they might make. Anna turned to Sam with a giggle. "Just wait a bit...they'll be asleep soon."

Mary and Sara drifted off to sleep with their hands clasped, not even the raging coastal storm could keep them awake for long. It had been a hard, but good day.

The family had enjoyed a great time unpacking their belongings. Each item brought some kind of a comment. Things like Anna's lace curtains now seemed frivolous while Sam's collection of rifles became much more appreciated. Yesterday, Anna had discovered that something had tried to get at the goats during the night. No wonder she'd heard frightened bleating in the early hours. Closer inspection led to the discovery of tracks and digging marks near the goat shed door. The tracks hadn't been that big. Sam had said they were definitely cat tracks.

Anna grew nostalgic as she emptied the box containing the kitchen stuff. Much of the baking equipment and all of the pots and pans had belonged to her grandmother. The cookware had appeared out of place in the city, but here it felt homey and fitting. Many of her old time recipes would come in very handy as supplies would be basic at the most. She was eager to try making sourdough starter from what they called wild yeast...then there was her grandmother's recipe for Johnny cake and of course the ones for venison.

"Hey, wake up, dream girl. Time's a wasting while you are off in la la land." Sam had come in for his lunch. He'd been digging over and extending the previous owner's garden plot. His hair and shirt were still damp from the water he'd poured over himself.

"Pretty darn hot today. Ground is nice and moist though. Digging is going well, even the untilled patch. Wish we'd brought a plow with us, but there just wasn't any room, as you know. If we keep at it every spring and toss in kelp, that ground should stay manageable. We'll rotate the crops like the book says. Should be fine." He sat down heavily.

Anna shrugged. "Don't know what you are so worried about as far as that garden is concerned. I had lots of experience growing stuff in Northern British Columbia. Not much different here, I expect. Just more rain and a soil that needs a helping hand. It looks like there are only a few inches of good soil and the rest of it is a mixture of rocks and clay. I think we are going to need to add that kelp for sure."

"Where are those daughters of ours? Not seen them all morning. They haven't been down at the rocks have they?" Anna looked at her husband.

"You have to learn to relax a bit more, girl. Both can swim and both of them have a good head on their shoulders."

"I know," she sighed, "but those cat tracks spooked me. This is such a peaceful place that it is hard to remember there can be danger."

"Tomorrow all of you girls are getting lessons on how to shoot the guns. Keeping a loaded shotgun over the front door will be a good idea, but everyone has to know how to handle firearms first." Sam reached around his wife's waist and drew her close. They stood in a warm embrace.

"What's for lunch?" Sara said as a squeaking hinge announced the girls. She was the picture of freedom with her cheeks ruddy from the wind and her hair framing her face with spiraling golden curls. Even Mary looked more relaxed. She had lost the pinched furrows between her eyes and that haunted gaze that dulled their blueness. Her disfigurement seemed less obvious since they had come to the homestead. All the outdoor work had begun to weather and tan her face. The bit of colour softened the stark contrast of her pale skin and the cruel reddish patch. Yes, it was still very noticeable, but to her family who were used to seeing her marred face, it became almost invisible.

Sam began to ladle his soup from the heavy tureen. Sharp, pungent aromas rose from his bowl, and mixed with the yeasty smell wafting from Anna's freshly baked rolls.

◇◇◇◇◇◇

Sara and Mary spent the evening hours constructing some very elaborate targets. Beside the goat shed, they made a couple of standing targets from driftwood and discarded bucket lids. Sheltered from the wind, these structures would be the first to be annihilated. Further up the steep bank leading to the creek, they fashioned a lumpy 'animal' out of sod, kelp and one of Sam's old shirts. However, their pride and joy was a row of tin cans perched on the rocks bordering their beach.

"Those are going to be hard," giggled Sara, "even for Dad." The cans were arranged at various angles, sometimes two or three deep.

"Mom will probably do pretty well," said Mary as she paused to brush the sand off her knees. "She is good at tennis, baseball and catch. She knows angles and stuff."

"Yup, but you know who I think will be the best? You… Mary. I think you are going to be the fastest learner."

Mary laughed. Her cheerful sound filled the growing dusk with lightness. "Me? I suck at just about every sport I've ever tried. Still you never know. Say let's make a bet. Whoever sucks the most has to do dishes for a week."

"You're on. Dad can choose the winner." Sara turned and raced up the trail towards the cabin. "Dad, Dad, you get to pick the winner. We have a bet."

Sam turned the edge of his page and put his paperback down on the grass beside his chair. He ruffled his oldest daughter's hair as she sank on her knees by his side.

"What are you on about now?" he said, smiling at the carefree lilt in his daughter's voice.

Sara explained their bet and told him in great detail how they had made the different targets. "We have to do the cans last, though. They're pretty hard, I think. Even you might have a bit of trouble."

"You never cease to amaze me, girl. Don't you have any faith in your old man? However, I'm betting on your Mom."

"How come no one ever bets on me?" complained Sara. She pouted and searched her father's eyes. "I don't need things as much as Mary, do I?"

"No, sweetheart, you don't. You are my brave girl, my dependable girl, my eldest. I know I can count on you. You'll never let me down will you?" With those words, he sealed her fate.

CHAPTER 10

KARL OPENED THE DOOR INTO THE SHARED BATHROOM. Unconsciously clenching his mouth as the usual mess assaulted him, he swore softly. That dickhead had left the toilet again. Was he brought up in a freaking barn or a pigsty? What does it take to remember to bloody well flush? He'd had it. Banging his fist on the adjoining door, he hollered, "Can't you at least flush the can after you take a dump? You frigging asshole. And don't you forget it's your turn to clean up in here. I did it last week."

A loud snorting came as Ren yanked the door open. "What the hell are you carrying on about now?" he snarled. "I was asleep, you dipshit."

"Shit is what I'm on about. For God's sake flush. Don't need to see what you ate last week, you constipated moron."

"Bugger off," came the curt reply, followed by the door almost unhinging itself from the force of the slam.

Karl couldn't win with this guy. At first he'd tried to be accommodating, tried to be friendly, but there was no getting any respect. He made up his mind to speak to Ralph, the camp foreman. Sure, it was a little thing, but it bugged the hell out of him. Maybe he could get moved to a different room. A room change might be highly unlikely. The camp was running at full capacity. Ren was due for his break next week. With any luck he wouldn't return.

Slowly Karl started down the hall towards the cleaning supplies. A clean bathroom was one of the things his mother had drilled into him. Even on the old homestead, everything had been kept as neat and tidy as possible.

The thought of his mother made him sad. She had always been his favorite parent, even after she'd broken his dad's heart. He'd hated her for leaving, but never blamed her for whatever had happened out there. He knew his dad had been hard to live with even before all the betrayals. Then afterwards, his father had taken his frustrations out on him. He swore under his breath as he remembered the silences, the shouting, occasional beatings and constant harping. Oh well, the stubborn old git was pushing up daisies now. Bending over he grabbed the cleaning supplies out of the cupboard.

As he scrubbed furiously at the bowl, he imagined the caustic blue gel congealing in Ren's throat. Serve the bastard right, wouldn't it? Too bad they were at this camp. Violence here automatically gained you a one way ticket home. Although the camp was far from being dry and the bosses seemed to turn a blind eye as to what went on in the furthest trailer, it was made very clear that you kept your hands to yourself. Just last month two of the younger fellas were turfed for fighting. No severance pay for either one. Good thing Ren enjoyed poker. Now he was going to pay big time.

He caught the warning glance from George as he swept the last of the chips his way. "Guess it wasn't your night, eh Ren? You and Big Joe seemed to back the wrong horse tonight, for sure."

Big Joe just shrugged. "Ah, you win some and you lose some. Tomorrow will be different. 'Bout time me luck changed for the better."

Ren glowered. He grabbed the cards and stared at the backs. "Don't know what's up, but something doesn't feel right," he muttered. He ran his fingernail over the back of a card. He examined his fingernail and the card. There was no residue. He looked at Karl and then at George. "There's something going on here. Can't quite figure it out, but something's rank... you cheating?"

"Christ, you are sure a sore loser," snickered Karl. "Don't hear you bellyaching when you're on the winning side."

Ren chucked the cards down and slammed his palm on the beer stained table. "Can't figure it out, but I will. And when I do there'll be hell to pay. No one cheats Ren Balderson, no one," he said menacingly. "Hell to pay," he threatened. With that he stumbled drunkenly out the door, falling down the last three entrance steps. "Hell to pay."

George shot another look at Karl and raised his hands. "Sore loser," he said to the other players, shrugging his shoulders. He got up. "You guys clean up. I'm bushed."

Catching a few hours shut eye was next on Karl's agenda. He lay fully clothed on his bed. Out of the corner of his eye, he saw a slight movement and then heard the click of the bathroom door lock. Each room had an adjoining passage to the shared washroom. The bathroom doors could be locked from inside and out if you wanted privacy. Raising his head from the pillow, Karl glanced around his room. He couldn't remember if he had locked that door before he'd gone to play cards. Then to his dismay, he saw the door to the closet was slightly ajar. His strong box. Leaping from his bunk, Karl tore open the closet door and discovered the box lying open on its side on the floor. The contents were strewn all over.

Someone had obviously been snooping. He counted the cash, inspected his remaining packages of marked cards and saw that the contacts were still in their vials. Nothing seemed to have been touched. Figuring he must have disturbed the snoop in the process, Karl gathered up his stuff and put it back into the grey metal container. As he shut the box, he discovered the lock had been jimmied. *Bloody hell*, he thought and then he shrugged. No matter. He could show Ralph the box and it would strengthen his request for a new room.

The clock showed six-thirty. It was time to head to the kitchen to prep breakfast.

As the bleary-eyed gamblers and the other men sauntered past his serving station, Karl looked hard at Ren. Ren smiled smugly. "There's hell to pay," he said in a voice that only Karl could hear.

Karl slapped the ladle of scrambled eggs down on Ren's plate so hard that the crack echoed throughout the mess hall. China shattered all over the floor and eggs spewed covering Ren's boots and jeans. "Sorry," snickered Karl. "Shame. That was the last of the eggs too." Flipping him the bird, he left to get the clean-up bucket.

Later, he stood in front of the office doorway. Smiling at Marilyn, he put in his request for a different room after the shift change. "I can't stand the son of a bitch. Filthy pig."

Karl chucked the damaged strong box onto her desk. "Need a new strongbox as well. Pretty sure he must have been in my room. See the lock is busted."

"Anything taken?" Marilyn asked as a worried frown crossed her face.

"Not that I know of, but you be sure to tell Ralph that I'm pretty damn sure it was Ren. When is the next crummy out of here? Maybe I'll sling my hook."

Marilyn shot Karl a concerned look. She knew that if he moved on, she'd be back to the mess hall. She hated the long hours of cooking and prepping.

"Don't be so hasty. Nothing that can't be fixed. Leave it to me. Don't want to lose my best buddy, now do I?" Getting up from behind the desk, she shuffled off into the storage room and came back with a new security box twice the size of the broken one.

"Here, will this do? It's got a combination lock as well. Better than that the one you got for sure." She smiled, looking at him from under her exaggerated lashes. She wasn't a bad looking woman for her age and she rather fancied the Swede. Most of the men around here had either two teeth or none. What she had with her boss, Ralph, was not much more than a grope and a feel every now and then.

"Great, thanks. Now you be sure and tell him what I said." Karl took the box, hurried out and over to his bunkhouse. He'd left the contents of the strong box on his bed. Although he'd secured the doors, he wanted to get the stuff put away before the men returned from the day's work in the bush.

He felt his every move being watched by more than just Ren; Karl trod carefully at the game that night. George had warned him that talk was making the rounds and a couple of the regulars were asking if he knew anything about someone fixing the games.

Slitting open a new deck, Karl did his shuffle and set out to deal. Ren won the first three games handily. Popping another cap, the mark drained his fourth beer. For a big man he was an easy drunk. His luck began to turn and Tim won the next few rounds.

George McKinnon lost steadily. Folding his hand, he threw in. "I'm done. You guys are too good for me tonight. Think I'll just watch and see Lady Luck smile on you losers for a change."

Karl worked his crowd, letting luck ebb and flow as it would in a regular game. As the men appreciated their beers and grew tired, they gradually threw caution to the wind and upped the ante. Nothing appeared to be dodgy. Karl carefully palmed the growing stack of cash and slid it under his butt. Out of sight out of mind was his motto.

The evening wore down and most of the men, including Ren were left with still a little of their cash. Not much, but a little.

"Better night, tonight," George said as he strode along beside Karl. "How much we clear anyway?"

"Better than three thousand I think, but I have to do the tally. Tomorrow's the last night before the crummy does the turn around. I'll take more chances then. I'm heading in on the next trip and will stash the takings in a locker at the bus station like we agreed."

◇◇◇◇◇◇

Karl stuffed most of the cash under the dirty work clothes in his bag and put the rest in his money belt. Climbing into the van, he gave a brief nod to the other men and settled in for the bumpy ride to town.

Out of the corner of his eye Karl saw it coming, but by then it was too late— way too late. Searing pain spread like molten lava erupting in rivulets of blood coursing down the angles of his face. Slowly turning his head back towards the source, he tried to focus on the arm attached to the fist. A row of brass knuckles and a flash of white teeth competed with manic laughter identifying his tormentor. Ren was enjoying this.

Desperately trying to deflect the blows, Karl rolled his body towards the vehicle's sliding door. As the van slowed, he managed to haul open the door and fall out onto the rough, muddy road bed. The ground rose to meet his outstretched arm snapping it like a rotten twig. Gritting his teeth against the pain, Karl fought to regain his wits. Shaking his head to clear his vision; he staggered to his feet. With his legs threatening to buckle, he lurched into the underbrush. Several yards away from the road, he scrabbled under a fallen log, hiding himself from view.

The van came to a screeching halt. Slamming doors and angry shouts seeped under the log, reaching Karl's ears in spite of his harsh wheezing. Willing his lungs to breathe slowly, he quietened his gasps and panted like a dog. His body relaxed and his breathing became inaudible. He was safe as long as they didn't upturn his sanctuary.

Moments dragged eternally. Footfalls echoed through the scrub. Dry leaves crinkled and rustled. Voices came and went. The searching men came up short. "Shit. Let's get out of here. The freaking bugs are eating me alive. Let's leave the son of a bitch to rot in the woods."

Ren snickered at Tim's suggestion. He'd clocked Karl a good one. He was hoping that with a little luck, the bastard would bleed to death and become animal fodder. "Yeah, let's go. He left the duffel in the van so we probably have the money anyway."

Eagerly Ren and his cohorts rifled Karl's bag and just as eagerly shared the loot.

"We'll have to get rid of this bag. Don't need any evidence left in the van. He might surprise us, live and go squealing to the cops. I sure as hell don't need cops sniffing around." Ren gathered up the strewn clothing and shoved it back into the duffel.

The last thing Karl heard as he lapsed unconscious was his duffel bag thwacking the dirt and the metallic grinding of gears as the driver gunned the van back into action. Black fingers closed his eyes and peaceful oblivion took over.

Chapter 11

SAM AND ANNA STOOD IN FRONT OF THE HOME HARDWARE STORE calendar they'd tacked to the wall beside the wood stove. It was the middle of June.

"Well, looks like we've broken the back of it. Garden's in, water's all set up, cabin is liveable and the animals are housed. I'd say we've done well in just these few weeks. It's time for a celebration. Time for a party!"

Anna grinned as she gazed at the satisfied smile on her husband's face. She agreed. They had all worked hard and had accomplished a great deal. "Yeah, we've done a lot. Still, there's much more to do before fall sets in, but we should have some fun. Let's make it a real surprise for the girls. You keep them away and busy for the day. I'll see what I can do."

◇◇◇◇◇◇◇

"Get up, sleepy heads."

Sam lounged against the doorframe set in the wall dividing the girls' room from the one he shared with Anna. He waited for the reluctant protests to come from his daughters. "Come on, get up, you two. I want to trek over the hill behind us and see how far we can go back into the woods before it gets too rough. The real estate map shows quite a trail back there."

Both girls shot out of bed eager to go on an adventure. They weren't allowed to venture far from the home site by themselves. They had explored just about every inch of the beach in front to the cabin, the hillside as far as the springhead and the cave.

"Don't we have stuff to do?" asked Sara as she stuffed her feet into her socks. "You said we were going to start on the woodpile next."

"Nah, I'm due for a break. Let's just spend the day enjoying ourselves," Sam said.

"Is Mom coming?" Mary wanted to know.

"No, we are going to leave her in peace. She is looking forward to a day without you monsters." Sam laughed throwing his arm around Mary's shoulders.

By the time the girls were dressed and had eaten their oatmeal, Anna had their knapsacks filled with lunch and bottles of water. Slapping hats on their heads, she ushered them out of the cabin. "Take care and don't get lost. Be back by at least five or I will start to worry." She hugged her husband close, "I love you".

◇◇◇◇◇◇

Anna glanced about the dim cabin. Suddenly she whirled around and grabbed the coffee pot off the stove and her mug from the counter. Easing the door open with her hip, she pushed her way outside and sat down at the rough-hewn table in their outdoor eating area. It was too nice of a day to be indoors and she had plenty of time.

She sat drowsily in the early morning sun surrounded by the damp forest and twittering birds. Suddenly, all went very quiet. Anna peered into the bush. Holding her breath she tried to see what had disturbed the birds. A slight movement in the shadows caught her eye. She shifted her position slightly. A deer bounded off into the depths of the forest. Laughing with relief, Anna sipped her now cold coffee. It could have easily been a cougar or whatever had disturbed the soil in front of the goat shed the other night. Deer she could handle.

Sinking into thought, Anna reflected on her life. Now that they had decided to make a new start in the wilderness, she felt happier and freer than she had in a long time. City life had been such a strain on the family. Sam had not been happy working for Nooms. She had felt stifled by the hurried bustle of their everyday lives. Having grown up on the farm in rural Peace River, she chaffed against the commercialism and noise of the urban environment.

True, Mary's horrible situation at school had been the turning point, but she knew that eventually they would have abandoned the city anyway. The only one she worried about was Sara. Were they pulling her away from her dreams of becoming an artist? Would she be able to find fulfillment in the bush? For now, Sara seemed content. She had her paints, charcoals and oils. She delighted in the ever changing seascape and had started to branch out with abstract renditions of familiar subjects such as the family, animals and still life. Not that she'd had much time lately to paint. Yes, they were all due for some fun. The party tonight would be a typical kitchen party with the four of them whooping it up.

Shaking herself out of her reverie, Anna rose and collected her cup and the coffee pot. She opened the cabin door and went reluctantly into the gloomy, cool shelter.

Soon the evening meal started to take shape. A damp cloth covered the crab cakes lying on the counter. Rice was ready to be washed and sifted. She dipped the lettuce into a pot of spring water and shook the sparkling drops out the doorway, making a monkey's wedding in the brilliant sunshine. She was proud of their first crop of lettuce from the garden.

Turning to the stove, she carefully measured goat's milk, tapioca, sugar and a touch of cinnamon into the saucepan. As she stirred the pudding carefully, she mentally took stock of their supplies.

Money was not going nearly as far as they had first thought. They had lots of staples, but these last few weeks had made a large dent in their supplies. She had badly underestimated what they would need to survive the coming winter. Everything had been a lot more expensive than they had imagined. She had been shocked at the prices for flour, sugar, seeds, fat, and tinned goods. Gasoline had been very costly too. Sam had used a lot for the chainsaw and occasionally they needed to run the generator for power if the solar batteries were low.

Mary's anti-anxiety drugs were very expensive. Perhaps she could be weaned off them if she continued to make progress. She was sleeping better and hadn't had those screaming attacks in the middle of the night for ages. Anna hated drugs. She had watched her aunt become dependent on Prozac. The sooner Mary was off the prescription drugs, the better. She'd look up some herbal remedies in her naturopathic cure book as soon as she had time. Surely some of those plants grew around here. She'd have to venture into the forest, but she could do it.

One thing that her mother had passed on to Anna was all the stories of the wild woman of the woods and sasquatches. The forest was a source of terror, fascination and comfort for Anna. It was a strange mixture of dread and enticement that threatened to overwhelm her if she allowed her imagination to stray.

Tasting the now thickening pudding, Anna added a touch more cinnamon and some vanilla. After filling each glass dish to the rim, she covered the dishes with another tea towel and set them to cool. Supper was done as far as it could be for now.

Dragging out her sewing box, she began to work on the patchwork quilts she was making for the girls' beds. Mary's favourite colours were blue and green. This cover was a delicate combination of those with touches of deep-purple and buttercup yellow. She fell asleep sitting in the rocker, needle in hand, with the wood in the stove dying in soft hisses.

◇◇◇◇◇◇◇

As Sam and the girls toiled up the hillside, the sun beat down on them warming their backs and reddening their forearms. "Hold up, girls. Drink some water and have a bit of a rest. No hurry. Glad we all have hats today."

"Oh," Mary said gazing out over the sparkling sea. "I can see the island today. I wonder what the old man is doing. Do you think he's lonely?"

The three of them sat looking toward Thoresen Island. It appeared to be floating gently on the crests of the waves. Seagulls soared above the white caps seeking fry swarming just below the surface.

"He could be, but we'll probably never know. Sun Soon-Chun said he was a grumpy old hermit who doesn't encourage visitors at all. They tried to dock there last year and he chased them off with his shotgun."

"Maybe he thought they were pirates come to find buried treasure," joked Sara getting up and dusting off the seat of her pants. "Come on, let's get going. I want to see what's over there beside that broken-off tree. Maybe it marks the spot. You know...for the buried treasure."

◇◇◇◇◇◇

Mary jumped up eager to carry on. It was turning out to be one of those special days. As she waited impatiently for her father to lead the way, she felt her shoulders relax and the threads of last night's dream loosen. Turning her face upward towards a screeching eagle, she followed its path as it rode the thermal. She was beginning to appreciate her freedom. Like the eagle, she was ready to spread her wings and embrace it.

"Come on, Mary," urged Sara. "Race you to the top."

◇◇◇◇◇◇

As they approached the cabin they were surprised to see it shrouded in darkness. Silence echoed through the homestead. The dying sun cast deepening shadows, everywhere.

"Mom. Mom," called Sara. "We're home."

Pushing through the cabin door the family paused to let their eyes grow accustomed to the dim interior. The wood stove glowed eerily and smells invited sampling. They stood beside the table.

"Wonder where she's got to?" Sam said. "I wonder where that gal of mine is?"

As if on cue, Anna stepped out from behind the kitchen cupboard banging pot lids together. "Welcome home...it's party time."

Soon everyone joined in banging pots and dancing around the inside of their rustic cabin. Not content with the limited space, they soon spilled out into the evening air.

Sam grabbed his shotgun and fired off a couple of shells. "Happy day! Happy day!" He yelled as he grabbed his wife's hands and twirled her in a circle.

"Your mom and I decided today is a day for celebration. We've made a lot of progress since we got here. Thank you, girls, for all your hard work. I'm proud of my women folk, very proud." Sam drew each one into a great big bear hug.

As the Lindholm family tucked into the feast Anna had prepared, they gazed happily around. Yes, indeed things were looking decent. Their cabin was now a home and life was good here in the wilderness.

Daisy, the milking goat, set to bleating; reminding Sara that chores were never done. "Hold on, Daisy. Let me finish my tapioca and then I'll milk you. Just wait a bit."

Later that evening, the family sat round the fire pit sipping hot chocolate. Bats were starting their nightly hunt and over in the distance, the first of the season's frogs were adding their voices to the cooling air. Sam brought out his guitar and gradually even Mary joined in serenading the haunting beauty that surrounded them.

CHAPTER 12

THE LAST THING KARL FELT LIKE DOING WAS CELEBRATING, UNLESS of course he was celebrating the fact he was still alive.

Sharp pain radiating from his right arm insinuated itself in his consciousness. As he tried to move, rough bark ripped at his shoulder giving him even more discomfort. He dropped his head back down on the mouldy leaves; giving into the waves of pain.

Feeling the cool evening dampness seeping under the log, Karl tried once again to get his bearings. His laboured breathing came in wet earthy gulps. He knew that he was in dire straits.

He listened carefully. A small stream gurgled as it wove its way through the moss. An evening bird chittered. Its lonely call echoed by another further away. Rustling leaves betrayed some small forest creature in search of its meal. Everything was amplified.

Karl shook his head clearing the last strangle hold of unconsciousness. Gritting his teeth against the pain shooting through his arm, he slid cautiously from beneath the fallen log. He waited half expecting a boot to suddenly connect with his head. Nothing.

The tiny trickling stream mocked the burning thirst searing his throat.

He raised his head in order to glance around the now still forest. Nothing. Grunting with effort, he tried to kneel, then to stand.

Dizzy, he reached out and grabbed onto a small sapling. It swayed, but held his weight. *Where were they? Where were Ren and his cohorts?*

Unable to stand the temptation any longer, Karl staggered, mindless of impending danger, towards the faint sound of water tumbling over rocks and down into the mossy undergrowth. Roots and vines failed to find purchase as his feet bruised their stems. Branches whipped at his bare head scratching his forehead and raking his arms.

Reaching out with his hand to clear away the debris lining the creek, he was forced to reconsider. His right arm dangled uselessly. Clumsily, he reverted to his less dominant hand and scrabbled away at the decaying leaves. Sinking down onto his belly, he thrust his face into the cooling liquid. He drank.

Rolling over to his back, Karl rested oblivious to the wetness wicking up through his jeans and t-shirt. He closed his eyes against the pain. Thoughts raced through his head. *Where were they? Christ his arm hurt! How could he get out of this fuck-up?*

His strong will and fighting spirit finally kicked in. Karl sat up and took notice of his surroundings. He guessed that the gravel road was not that far away. He had taken off running after his tumble from the van, but he had been in no shape to make it very far.

He listened carefully. The forest was holding its breath. Gradually peace returned and birds began to dart at evening insects. The stream trickled gently and he could hear a faint buzzing in the bushes. Straining his ears, he searched the air for sounds of footsteps, the rumble of an engine or a dreaded human voice.

Satisfied that he was truly alone, Karl took stock of his predicament. His arm was badly broken. A compound fracture, if he remembered the first aid lessons his father had drilled into his unwilling brain. He actually felt something akin to gratitude as he thought of his father's lessons.

The old man had been cautious. He had made sure the entire family was knowledgeable about safety, first aid and what could be gleaned from the woods. Living on their isolated homestead, had meant that everyone had to be self-sufficient. Injuries and sickness had to be dealt with promptly. Infection could set in quickly and without intervention could mean loss of mobility or even death. Help had been many hours away from their West Coast property.

Karl grunted as he yanked on his wrist, straightening the exposed bone. Nauseated, he retched into the bushes. Gripping his shirt sleeve, Karl tightened the denim to stem the blood seeping from the aggravated wound. With his left hand, he undid his leather belt and then extracted his knife from its pouch.

It took him a good twenty minutes to hack a section of bark from the nearest birch. Pausing to retch once again, he wiped his mouth. Karl managed to splint his arm with the bark and fashioned a sling using his belt. It was a makeshift fix, but his arm felt much better when it wasn't flapping uselessly at his side.

The sun set plunging the woods into darkness. The combined shock of the beating, his broken arm and his predicament began to chill Karl's body. Staggering on unsteady legs, he set off in the general direction of the gravel road. He soon realized that travel was next to impossible. He couldn't determine in which direction to go. He needed to wait until daylight. With his back against a stump, Karl dozed on and off throughout the night. Each rustle, each scraping, each animal call brought him instantly alert.

The next morning, soft dewdrops dribbling from an overhead spruce woke Karl. Rubbing his eyes, he clambered to his feet. He felt miserable. His whole body ached from the damp, cold night and the bruises inflicted by Ren and his buddies. Only movement would help, so he shuffled off along the path in what he hoped was the direction of the gravel road.

CHAPTER 13

SUDDENLY ALL HELL SEEMED TO BREAK LOOSE. KARL SNAPPED HIS head around trying to identify where the shot had come from. Ducking behind the nearest fir, he waited.

"Son of a bitch. What are you doing on my land? Come on out, you Commie bastard."

Karl looked at the barrel of the rifle and at the wild-eyed creature that was at the other end. *Was it a man or a woman?* He couldn't tell.

"I said for you to come out. Git out where I can see you proper."

Karl raised his one arm and slid out from behind the skinny tree. He was no match for this threat. Swaying unsteadily on his feet he stood, as best he could, to face his opponent.

The rifle butt connected with the side of his head. The last thing he felt before plunging into unconsciousness was his body landing full force on his injured arm.

◇◇◇◇◇◇

Something warm caressed his forehead. A soft humming filled the air. He became aware that he was not alone. He could smell wood smoke, some kind of meat cooking and the unmistakable odour of his unwashed body.

"Welcome to the land of the living. You've been down a long time. I reckon you had one hell of a fever from the infection in your arm. What you wash it with? Swamp water?"

He tried to form words, but his tongue felt like matted hair plugging up his throat.

"Here, sip this."

Once again he tried to speak. This time he managed. "Thank you."

"I asked you what you cleaned your wounds with?"

He turned his head and stared at the woman who held the chipped cup to his mouth. It was hard to determine her age. If he had to guess, he'd say about fifty. Her hair framed her face with a wild halo of reddish-gold. Sea-green eyes peered at him from a pretty enough face. Wrinkles and sunburn swept across her face giving her a leathered look. Her lips were full and pouty.

"Just water, water from a stream. Who are you and where am I?" Karl demanded.

"All in good time. You are safe enough here if you behave yourself. Looks like someone laid a good beating on you. You running from the law?"

"No, robbed and dumped out of a van. The law had nothing to do with it."

The woman smiled for the first time. "Good. I'm not a fan of the law."

Karl glanced around him seeing a rough wood shack with a dirt floor and a barrel heater in the middle of the only room. It was sparsely furnished with the bare minimum of essentials— a plank table, a couple of stumps for chairs and the cot he was occupying. As his eyes grew accustomed to the gloomy interior, he realized that this woman actually lived in this space. It was rustic, but comfortable enough. Books lined a shelf beside the bed, tins of what must be food stuff were stacked near the stove and a couple of hooks on the door held jackets and other outdoor garments.

"You live here?" he asked tentatively. He didn't trust his nurse in the slightest. He felt the lump on his forehead where the gun had made its connection. "Ouch." Wincing at the tenderness he refocused his eyes. "Why in hell did you hit me?"

"Wasn't sure who you were or where you'd come from. I don't trust men, especially near my claim."

"Was I looking like a robber? Was I? Christ I was hardly making it down the trail."

"Yeah, I guess I just wanted to hit someone," smirked his unlikely saviour. "You were on my land and that makes you fair game." She moved over to the doorway and chucked the pan full of dirty warm water out of the cabin.

Handing him a small bowl, she ordered, "Here, get some of this soup down you and then we'll get you cleaned up. You smell worse than a packrat."

Sipping from his bowl of broth, Karl once again tried to make conversation. "What's your name?"

"Beth, short for Marybeth. Yours?"

Hesitating for a moment, Karl thought hard. Should he risk giving his true name or make something up? She looked tough, but there was something about those startling green eyes that belied her true nature. If he worked his magic, this one would succumb to his charms quite quickly. "Karl, Karl Thoresen."

"Well Karl, let's get you cleaned up. You're polluting my atmosphere. Mind you, if you try anything, I'll be burying your sorry ass."

After pouring a couple buckets of water into a huge pot that took up most of the stove top, Beth threw a grey threadbare towel in his general direction.

"When this heats up enough, git yourself on the other side of all that dirt. You'll find some duds in the box under the bunk. Should fit you...you're not much bigger than that son of a bitch husband of mine. Got to go check on a few things." Grabbing the rifle propped up near the door, she left.

Not ten minutes later, Karl heard her return. "Hey, I'm not decent yet."

Beth stopped short of the makeshift door. "Modest are we? Seen bigger than you, I expect." She settled down on a stump just outside the opening.

Karl's head shot up as he heard the rifle cock. A shot echoed through the forest. Obviously 'Annie Oakley' was target shooting or had just bagged supper. Shrugging, he turned his attentions to getting rid of the dirt, blood and muck that had accumulated over the last few days.

His cuts were scabbed over and were well on their way to healing. His arm had been reset; splinted with two short pieces of wood and some kind of sacking. *When had this all happened? How long had he been in this shack?* His forehead hurt, but it was the dull ache of bruised flesh curing.

Kneeling down gingerly, he managed to rummage in a box of clothing that had been stuffed under the bed. Sorting through the assortment of unisex gear, Karl found a pair of gitch, a red flannel shirt and a worn pair of jeans that only came halfway down his shins. Beggars can't be choosers he said to himself as he pulled on some thick woollen socks.

Finishing up, he yelled to the silent sentinel outside the door. "Shall I wash my clothes in the dirty water on the stove?"

"Yup, be a hell of a good idea."

Later that evening as they sat outside, they had relaxed enough around each other to start swapping a little information. Both of them held back; both told the other just the bare truth, no details.

As the night wore on, Karl felt exhausted. "Gotta get some shut eye. Where do you want me to bunk down?"

"You take the bunk for now. I'm set up over there by the stream."

Turning his head, Karl could just see a small pup tent nestled in amongst the bushes beside the path leading to the creek. Too tired to argue, he slowly got up and entered the shack. "Night and thanks. I reckon you saved my life. I owe you big time."

As the days turned into weeks, an easy truce sprung up between the two of them. His arm was mending; his bruises and cuts were hardly visible. Karl, now that he was healed enough, slept on the dirt floor using an old sleeping bag for cover.

Gradually he learned more about this woman of the woods. She had met and married a mountain man. When she had unfortunately shot and killed her husband in a hunting accident, she had gone a little bushed. She chose to remain here in the woods, hiking out only for supplies and the occasional medical appointments.

Since she had never reported his death, she was now paranoid of the law. This wild woman had survived alone for the last ten years. No wonder she seemed more than a little crazy.

Karl was amazed to see how self-sufficient she was. Her shack, although crowded with the two of them, was sufficient for her needs. She had dug a root cellar into a hillside and that was where she kept most of her food supplies. At any given time there was moose, deer or fish stashed in this cache. A small garden had been scratched in the shallow forest floor. Although it was early in the season, he could see the beginnings of her winter staples poking up from the ground. A small woven structure was the home for five hens and a rooster. This ingenious contraption gave the chickens freedom to scrounge for food during the day and could be closed in and hauled up a tree at night. He hadn't yet seen any likely predators, but it was a safe bet that fox, coyote and even bear might be attracted by the fowl. So far he hadn't discovered if the clever chicken coop and the root cellar were Beth's or her husband's doing, but given her prowess with the rifle and such, he wouldn't discredit her. She was one tough broad.

Admiration welled up in Karl as he thought about her unique lifestyle. He learned that she travelled several miles along forestry roads to get other supplies from the nearby town of Brookfield at least twice a year. This woman had made a cosy nest for herself in the middle of nowhere. Carefully camouflaged, her cabin was nearly impossible to see. If the rifles, shotgun and rows of ammo lined up beside the cabin door were any indication, she was well armed. She knew the ways of the bush, which medicinal plants to use, and how to hunt and fish. His tough, back-to-the-land, pioneering father would have been very impressed by Beth.

In the days that followed, Karl used a lot of the skills taught to him by his father. He built a drying rack and showed Beth how to cure venison with wild herbs. He made her a small fish smoker that they set up far away from the main camp for fear of attracting bear. By making himself useful, he knew he was gradually gaining her trust.

The one thing he was curious about was this claim that she occasionally referred to. This area was known for some pretty good strikes, but the surrounding streams did not appear to be dredged or worked in any way. She kept her claim location to herself. Twice, she had disappeared overnight coming back early the next evening and going straight to the root cellar. During one of her disappearances he had carefully searched the root cellar, but was unsuccessful in discovering any secret stash. He'd been apprehensive as well, not knowing when she was likely to return.

Later one evening as they sat chatting around the small outdoor fire, he led the conversation around to mining, gold and claims. "I was thinking of trying my luck at panning. Do you know any streams that might be good for a first timer like me? You could give me a demo. Never panned before, except this once, at some historic site in the Cariboo. It was very touristy."

"Panning's hard work. Time consuming as well," she said glancing at him through the frizzy halo that constantly framed her wrinkled face. "You'd be better off to stake a claim and then get an outfit. Sluice box is the best way. You can pick up the equipment easily enough from miners that have given up."

"Sure like to try panning though. Give me a couple of lessons?"

"It might be fun. Your arm's nearly mended. Let's wait a bit and I'll take you after I get back from going to town for supplies at the end of the week. Unless you want to hike out with me and be on your way."

"If it's all the same to you, I'd like to stay for a while longer. I've got nowhere to go in a hurry. Should lay low for a bit. Those guys may still be looking for me and I've no hankering for another beating."

"You never did tell me the whole story. What in hell did you do?"

Karl stood up and wandered over to the wood pile. He took his time selecting a couple of suitable logs. "Sometime...sometime, I'll fill you in. Too nice an evening for that kind of thing. Let's break out that last bottle of bourbon. I'll give you some of that cash in my money belt to buy more booze in town."

Beth brought out a bottle and they shared some of the booze, passing it back and forth. As the evening drew to a close, their inhibitions fell by the wayside.

She's a nice looking woman even if she's older than I'm used to, Karl thought to himself. Casually sliding his log over her way, he took a chance and reached for her hand.

Surprisingly, Beth didn't move away. She merely glanced in his direction. "It's been a long while for me, you know," she said in a voice that was scarcely above a whisper. "Not since that son of a bitch husband of mine took the bullet."

Karl didn't miss a beat. "Well, let's see if we can remember what to do, shall we? Not like we're virgins or anything."

Beth snorted with laughter and dragged him into the cabin. "You better be worth it. My old man wasn't much in the sack."

Later, Karl simply asked, "Well, worth crossing over to the dark side?"

Beth grabbed him again.

Chapter 14

SAM WAS SITTING ON A LARGE DRIFTWOOD LOG, LOOKING OUT TO sea, counting his blessings. It had taken them just over two years to bring his dream to life. In those two years, they had established quite a home for themselves. He smiled as he thought of the cabin, animal shelters and garden patch. He was satisfied that the wood piled high against the south wall of the cabin was sufficient for the coming winter months.

"Come sit with me," he called as he caught sight of his wife as she left the outhouse. He was even pleased with the way that had turned out. By following plans, he had been able to construct it and then power the composting unit using two solar panels mounted to the building's sloping roof. The door had a cut out of a face with one of its eyes winking. Chuckling to himself, he remembered when Mary had joked that she was off to visit 'winkie'. The name had stuck for good.

"You've nothing to do?" Anna lowered herself down beside Sam, wiggling a bit to move him over. "You could always weed the garden for me if you like."

"Nah, I just want to sit and stare out at that magnificent view. We are so lucky. So lucky."

Resting her head on his shoulder, Anna followed his gaze out over the seascape. "Sure is beautiful today. No fog or anything. I can just make out Thoresen Island. Often wonder about the old man."

"Yes," replied Sam lazily. "I think about him too. I'd find it dreadful to live alone like that. Suppose it must suit him or he wouldn't do it. Glad I have you girls to share paradise with." He squeezed her shoulders and planted a kiss on top of her head. "We've done alright wouldn't you say, old girl?"

"Yes, but I wonder how long we can keep this up without running out of ready money. You know we can't touch the girls' trust. We promised Mom."

"Next year we can try growing wheat. I was thinking of clearing a patch beside the creek just before it runs down over the hill. It would save a ton if we didn't need to buy flour. If we tapped some of those birch trees in the spring, we could even supplement our sugar."

Anna laughed. She was used to Sam and his ideas. "Yeah, but that wouldn't fix the lumber, medicine and booze problems. Mary's pills cost a small fortune and they don't even seem to do much good. Then again, I've been reading in the survival book that a few of the plants growing in the woods around here have calming qualities. Think I will stew some into a tea and give it to her, during the next episode."

"Wouldn't hurt to try. But you have to admit Mary's a lot better here. We haven't seen as much withdrawal and her outbursts are nearly non-existent. Just those damn nightmares."

"Sara seems good too. Did you see her painting of the eagle on the rock? I'm glad she has a bit more free time to explore her talent. That picture is great."

Sam smiled ruefully. "We've come too far to turn away now. Things will work out. You'll see."

◇◇◇◇◇◇

The wind was picking up. White caps foamed as they crested and broke over the rocks guarding the sheltered bay in front of the homestead.

Sara let out a holler as she glimpsed the distant shape of a fish boat as it rode the now heaving seas. "Someone's out there in this weather. Looks like they are coming this way."

The family gathered on the cliff top. Watching through binoculars, Sam could tell the vessel was struggling to make headway. Even in these seas, a fish boat should make better time than the craft seemed to be doing. As the boat gradually came closer, they recognized the Korean flag flying from the wheelhouse. Several of the crewmen were waving and a familiar voice called out. "Sam, Anna, hello. Sun Soon-Chun very glad to see you."

After all the smiles and handshakes, the family led the Koreans up towards their cabin. Anna had put on a huge pot of soup as soon as they had realized the vessel was in trouble and heading towards their cove. "Come along quickly. Let's get you warmed up and fed," insisted Anna as the weary sailors hung back shyly. "There's a lot to eat. Come on, come on."

Hungry and exhausted from battling the heavy seas, under half-power, for hours; Soon-Chun and his men scarfed down the soup and hot tea. Apparently the engine repair, done in Seattle, had not held.

Sam, Sun Soon-Chun and the first mate Shin Jorg-Kyi were soon deep in discussions of engine repairs, parts and money. Sun Soon-Chun made no secret of how he felt about the Americans that had cheated him in the Seattle boat yard. "I no trust them. No good buggers."

Sam, always one to give the benefit of the doubt, argued that perhaps it was not being cheated, but an honest mistake. "Here, let me have a look. Perhaps I can figure out what's wrong."

Sun Soon-Chun grinned at his first mate. "I told you Sam would fix. Told you."

After spending most of the night and the entire next day hunched over the old engine, Sam succeeded in getting it running properly. The crew took it out of the bay to be sure the fix held this time. As the vessel tied up once again to the Lindholms' dock, cheers rang out from the crew.

Sun Soon-Chun insisted on bringing ashore huge bottles of Soju and the party that ensued had no rival. Once the Koreans got into the booze, they showed a gregarious side that surprised everyone. Much singing, laughter and hilarious attempts to speak English emerged.

Shin Jorg-Kyi took his captain aside and spoke for a long time. Beckoning to Sam, they then included him in their discussion. In spite of their limited English, it was clear that they were offering Sam a job. They wanted him to fish with them the next season. His MacGyver-like skills had impressed them. They needed his talents and Sam needed their money.

Sam and Anna discussed the deal. For two months in the early spring and for the salmon season, late August to sometime in October, Sam would fish for the Koreans and do engine and equipment repairs. In exchange, Sam would earn more than enough to purchase the homestead supplies without having to tap into the girls' trust funds. It seemed like an answer to their dilemma.

"I'm not crazy about you going off and leaving me here on the homestead alone with the girls," Anna worried. "What if something happens to one of them?"

"It could happen if I were here as well," countered Sam. "You can cope. I know you can. Besides, let me try it for the spring season. I can always quit if it's too much."

Knowing that their dream was in danger if Sam didn't take this opportunity, Anna reluctantly agreed. With a handshake the deal was done. Sun Soon-Chun and his crew departed on the next tide with promises to return in the spring.

Anna watched them go, trying to ignore the knot of worry in her gut.

Throughout that fall and winter Sam made sure the womenfolk were able to do everything that was required to run the homestead without him. He taught them how to hunt, skin and prepare the small dog-sized deer that roamed the island. Sara was squeamish at first, but soon became a crack shot. She was able to skin and cut up a deer in less than a day. Mary turned out to be excellent at fishing. She enjoyed the solitude than came with the waiting for the fish to bite.

It was more difficult to teach his girls how to repair the water system and the other machinery, but he rationalized that if it was in good repair before he left not much could go wrong. There was always the old method of hauling buckets of water from the creek if all else failed. He intended to have most of the wood cut, but Anna and Sara could easily handle the axe. Anna was better than he was in an emergency, and she knew more about medicines and first aid.

Admitting to himself that Anna would be lonely, he took comfort in the fact that the girls were well behaved and would be no trouble to their mother. Mary's episodes were fewer and becoming less intense. Sara could calm her down without too much effort. Those daughters of his had such a special bond. Yes, he acknowledged his home would survive his departure for a few months at a time. He'd probably suffer the most living on the boat, eating Korean food and drinking that gut rot they called Soju. He'd miss his family and this little piece of paradise they called home.

True to their word, the Koreans returned the following spring. With lingering hugs and promises to be careful on all sides, Sam slung his duffel onto the deck. He reached for Anna once more and then he was gone.

The girls waved and waved until the fish boat was a mere memory on the horizon.

CHAPTER 15

KARL GAVE BETH HALF AN HOUR TO BE GONE DOWN THE TRAIL. She would be back in three days, four at the most.

When he was absolutely sure she had made it far enough down the path so as not to bother returning for anything she'd forgotten, he began searching her property. The gold had to be somewhere. The previous night, she had shown him some of the nuggets she was cashing in this trip.

"My God," he had exclaimed as he gazed at the dull lumps of heavy gold. "How much is that all worth?"

"Depends on the current price for gold on the market," she explained. She implied that she was expecting at least a couple of hundred dollars.

"How long did it take you to dredge that? That's not all of your winnings is it?"

The smile on her face had told him her answer.

Now, he was going to find the cache if it was the last thing he'd do. He closed his eyes and tried to visualize where someone would hide gold nuggets. Most of the nuggets weren't all that big, but it would have to be somewhere very secure. Somewhere no one would go looking.

He hadn't noticed when she had retrieved the gold. In fact, he had no idea exactly when she had gotten it. All of a sudden, she had just shown him the nuggets. There they were nestled in the palm of her hand.

Gold was the answer to his prayers. Gold was his ticket to paying off George's boss. He owed most of the money that the men had ripped off him. That money in the duffel bag had not been all his… most belonged to the syndicate. He couldn't resurface in town until he'd squared away his debt. He needed a stake as well.

With his eyes still closed, he mentally flew over the tiny homestead. Bit by bit, he let his mind filter the possibilities. The banks of the creek seemed too obvious. He hadn't seen her looking or scrabbling around in the cabin or the tiny yard.

Jumping up from the stump chair, he searched her jackets, boots and the band of her husband's bush hat. Nothing. Gingerly he felt around the back of the wood stove and where the chimney rose up through the shack's roof. Zilch. Then turning his attention to the lean-to that served as the outhouse, he explored every nook and cranny.

He let his eyes scan for signs of loose dirt around the tree trunks. He searched. His gaze fell on that ingenious chicken coop. Of course, that had to be it. No one would think of the chicken coop. Besides, those bloody birds were pretty wild pecking at anyone but Beth.

He quickly overturned the rain barrel, draining the water. Steeling himself against the furious pecks, he caught each of the five hens and the rooster. He shoved them unceremoniously head first into the barrel. The squawking ceased abruptly when he threw an old tarp over the opening, plunging the chickens into darkness.

Feeling with his hands, Karl searched the coop. On the underside, he felt a thicker piece of wood. One of the slats was double. Prying open the join, he discovered a hollow neatly carved into both pieces of wood. The ensuing cavity held three small pouches. "Yes!" Karl's hands shook as he ripped open all three cloth bags. Nuggets fell like hail onto the dusty ground. He was looking at a fortune. He was looking at his salvation.

Shrugging off any regretful feelings, Karl breathed in deeply. *Sure, she was a nice piece of tail. She'd probably saved his life. But, he didn't owe her a damn thing, not really. He'd miss her infectious laugh and he had grown to like her. Still, life moved on and he was a free agent. She'd never leave the bush anyway. To hell with her...she'd survive.*

Tossing the chickens back into their coop, he tried to make everything look the same as it had before. He changed out of the borrowed clothes and put on the jeans and shirt that he'd arrived in. As he packed his bag, he slowly glanced around what had become his home in the last while. The bed they'd shared, the crude table where she'd served up her spicy concoctions and the guns lined up beside the door accused him. *Bloody hell.*

Guilt shot arrows into his heart. Confident she would be working her claim soon, he took only three quarters of the gold, leaving Beth enough to get by on. He estimated his share was at least six grand.

Shouldering his pack, he set off up the same trail she'd followed a scarce three hours before. When he reached the tree where Beth had first accosted him, he turned to the right, heading away from the gravel road. Judging by the lay of the land, he figured he might make those distant hills by night fall. He knew that beyond the hills, a criss-cross of trails would lead him to the lake beside the work camp. He'd have to make sure to keep well away from the camp. His plan was to meet up with some of those sports fishermen. He hoped it would only be a matter of time before he could persuade one of them to give him a ride back into civilization.

He was still trudging through the bush when night fell swiftly shrouding the scrubland in dark shadows. The big dipper appeared overhead and to the left a series of stars pointed to the east. Breathing a sigh of relief, he understood that he was on the right track for the lake. Since darkness was hindering his progress, he found the nearest fir; sat down and leaned his back against its trunk. Throwing his jacket over his knees, he dozed off fitfully throughout the night. As morning approached, he once again headed towards the distant hills.

Towards mid-day, Karl crested the last hill and saw the lake spread out like a jewel in front of him. At the head of the lake, he could see the smoke rising from the work camp's stove and could hear the occasional sounds of human voices. Keeping close to the cover of the trees, he made his way down to the water's edge. Over to the right were remnants of a campfire, a small tent and skid marks made by someone dragging a boat into the water. A beat up pick-up truck was parked at the end of the rutted road. He gathered some dry wood and began to rebuild the fire.

"Hello, there," Karl called as soon as the runabout came into view.

"Oh, great, company!" The young man steering the boat seemed less than thrilled to see their camp occupied. Killing the outboard, he bumped the boat up onto the shore. He jumped out and turned to give his girlfriend a hand getting out of the runabout. "Who in hell are you?" he demanded as they strode purposefully into their campsite.

Karl smiled his best smile and held out his hand. "Karl, Karl Thoresen."

Taken back by this stranger with good manners, the young couple stared.

"Sorry to come by unannounced," Karl added. "My car broke down on the gravel road and I hiked in to see if I could catch a ride into town with one of you fishermen."

"You hiked in all that way," the tiny blonde exclaimed as she sat down on one of the logs that lined the campfire. "That sure is a long way. We came in by the short cut. Rough as all get out, but the truck's a wreck anyway."

"Yup, I reckon I could've got to town and back by the time I slashed through all that devil's club." Karl pulled up a pant leg to show the young couple his badly stung leg.

"Shit, that's nasty. I'm Susan and this here's Tom, Tom McBride. I've got some cream for that leg."

"Great and I got some of this to share," Karl grinned pulling out the last of the Kentucky bourbon that he'd taken from Beth's. He saw their eyes light up at the sight of the liquor. He'd have no trouble catching a ride with these two.

Three days later, the young couple was ready to abandon camp and head back to their boring nine-to-five jobs in Vancouver. Karl found himself in their clapped-out beater bouncing along the rutted goat path that passed for an access road. The campers had been right. The truck was on its last legs. He doubted the springs would last much longer and by the sound of the transmission, it was dying as well.

The outskirts of Vancouver eventually came into view. Tom was forced to limp the gas guzzling, oil spewing truck into the nearest gas station with a mechanic's bay.

He disappeared into the garage with the owner. Several minutes later he reappeared shaking his head in disbelief. "Tyler says the only thing this truck is good for is the wreckers. It will cost too much to fix, but we might get some cash if we salvage parts."

Susan looked at him and sighed. "Well, can't say we didn't know it was toast. What are we going to do? I've got to be at work on Monday."

Karl seized his opportunity. "Listen, I got a few bucks…enough for bus fare for the two of you. Sign the truck over to me. I'll stay and junk her. I can send you the money minus the bus fare of course."

After much whispering and discussion between the two of them, Tom and Susan decided to take Karl up on his offer.

Tom shrugged his shoulders. "Hey man, we have no choice. We don't have enough money for the bus ourselves so we'd be glad to make the deal. Not like we're strangers anymore."

Karl grinned. "Nah, three days in the bush together makes us practically kin. Don't worry. If you give me your bank account number, I can deposit the funds as soon as I get the cash for old Betsy. What about the boat? It's still pretty good."

"Yeah, the boat," said Tom ruefully. "It was my old man's and I'd hate to part with it. Let's see if there is a storage place around here. We can come back for it."

At the bus station, Tom shook Karl's hand. "Thanks man, for all you've done. Thanks."

Susan threw her arms around the Swede and kissed his check. "Take care. See you."

Karl waved as the bus drew onto the highway. Turning towards the garage, he sauntered over to retrieve the pick-up. Three cranks and she fired up, spewing a cloud of blue.

The wrecker's yard was six clicks back on the highway. He managed to get three hundred bucks for the truck. Karl knew that was too little, but he wasn't about to dicker. He had places to go and gold to sell.

After finding the nearest Bank of Commerce, he transferred two hundred and thirty dollars into Tom's account. He withdrew the last of his own funds from the ATM. Crossing the street, he checked into the hotel attached to the Royal Casino. First, get some sleep; then to sell those nuggets; followed by some Lady Luck.

Chapter 16

IN THE EARLY SUMMER EVENINGS, IT BECAME THE GIRLS' HABIT TO sit on the rocks lining their beach, and look out over the ocean. Since they had no way of knowing when their father would return, it became a way for them to feel less lonely. Occasionally, Anna would join them but more often than not she enjoyed some time by herself.

In early June, just as the sun was lowering in the evening sky, Mary let out a yell. "He's coming. He's coming."

Sure enough a boat was forging its way towards their sheltered bay. As it drew closer all doubt disappeared. The distinctive Korean flag, with its white background, red and blue taegeuk centered and black trigrams in the corners, was clearly visible. Sam and Sun Soon-Chun stood at the bow, their faces wreathed in huge grins.

With no time to waste, Sun Soon-Chun anchored off shore and sent Sam ashore in the tender. The boat's hold was full and he was anxious to make Prince Rupert before the fish spoiled.

Sam tossed his bag onto the dock, jumped and landed in the welcoming arms of his daughters. With a quick shove he sent the tender back towards the waiting vessel.

Anna was coming down the path. Her hair picked up the last rays of the sun and her smile lit her tired face. "Welcome home,

Sam. Welcome home," she whispered as he held her tightly. "I'm so glad you're home. I've missed you so much."

A shy smile crossed her face. Sam looked at her intently. "What's up, girl?"

She gave him a coy look and laughed. Sam laughed with her. He reached for Anna again.

◇◇◇◇◇◇

As Sam reeled in his line, he thought about the last three years. Sighing, he watched as an eagle flew low over the cliffs. Disappointed that they had not reached total self-sufficiency, he tried to justify his absences. Yes, Anna was dreadfully lonely when he was off fishing, but if they were to continue living here, they had to get money somehow. Perhaps now that she was pregnant again things might be better. A baby would fill her lonely days. He knew his girls were content and settled into their lifestyle. Each season brought new challenges, routines and variety to their world. Three years had passed quickly.

Sun Soon-Chun had been very good to him. Smiling, he remembered the nights drinking Soju aboard the fish boat. Man, that guy could drink anyone under the table. After each spring session, Sun Soon-Chun would convert Sam's earnings for the year into supplies for the coming months. The captain ordered the supplies once he reached port. He meticulously followed Anna's detailed list and returned with the goods when he came for Sam in the fall. The supply shipments were working out very well.

Frowning, Sam got up and gathered the rest of his fishing gear. He did not miss the city life at all, but he knew Anna sometimes longed for her mother and some of the few friends she'd had at work. The first thing she asked the crew of every boat that called in was, "Any mail?" Sun Soon-Chun or the Coast Guard vessel occasionally brought letters that would be read over and over again.

Sam drew his coat closer around his wiry frame and jammed his woolen cap firmly on his head. The heightened smell of salt on the quickening breeze indicated a storm was brewing somewhere out in the Pacific. Striding towards the cabin, he began whistling. He checked the sheds and dragged the chairs in under the cabin's overhanging roof for protection. "Anna, where are the girls? There's a storm coming. I can feel it."

"Sara's here, but I think Mary's in her hidey-hole…the cave. Probably lost track of time again. I'll send Sara."

"Nah, I'll get her. Christ, I wish she wouldn't disappear like this." Slipping a bit on the steep path leading to the cave, Sam steadily climbed the hill. The wind had really increased and it was only a matter of time before rain would be lashing at the cabin windows.

He puzzled about his youngest daughter. Mary's mental state remained quite stable with only minor flare-ups whenever fishermen or the Coast Guard called in at the island. When strangers came, or if she was anxious, she had developed a habit of quietly disappearing. She would retreat to the cool cave and sit on one of the barrels, humming to herself. Her humming and the noise from gulls and wind must help her block out intrusive thoughts.

He reached the entrance of the cave and peered inside. There she sat huddled in a blanket amidst the apple barrels, potato bins and shelves lined with produce Anna and Sara had put up last fall. Feeling frustrated, Sam spoke abruptly. "Come on, girl. It's late and the storm is almost here."

Mary startled and let out a gasp. With her pale face betraying her torment, she stared vacantly, unable to remember where she was. As her father waited, she slowly returned to the present, away from Sharon's taunts. Sam watched her unconsciously reach up and touch her marked cheek. Tears stole down her cheeks.

Sam reached out and took his daughter into his arms. He knew she couldn't help her condition, whatever it was. Those doctors that they had taken her to, just before they had bought this homestead, couldn't really pinpoint her problem. Yes, they knew it was related to the severe bullying she'd suffered, but she didn't present enough symptoms to be diagnosed with post-traumatic stress syndrome. Besides, very little was known about this condition in young children. She was responding to antidepressants, so they felt it was just a matter of time before she recovered her mental health.

Looking around at what Mary considered her refuge, Sam wasn't sure. He was glad they lived in isolation. The next trauma or bullying might have easily sent Mary over the edge. As it was, they managed her immediate environment as best they could. They no longer polluted her system with those antidepressants the doctors had prescribed. Both he and Anna detested pharmaceuticals; preferring natural cures. Once again he was thankful that their eldest, Sara, could calm her sister if need be.

"It's all right, little one. It's okay." Sam held Mary's hand firmly as they made their way down to the cabin.

"She's here," called Sam. "But she's in a state. Sara, see what you can do."

Sara glanced at her father and then at Mary. As usual, she was the only one who could settle her sister. Gently, she drew Mary into their bedroom, undressed her as if she were five years old and tucked her into bed. Soon a tuneless lullaby could be heard as Sara sang her sister to sleep.

Sam looked at Anna. "At least Sara seems content here. Mary is safe. And now there's another on the way. Boy or girl? What do you think?"

Anna smiled softly and patted her small bump. "I've been so sick and tired this time. Not like with the girls…I'm thinking a boy…a little Samuel."

"Let's hope the baby arrives while I'm still here this spring. I know we've gone over all the emergency drills, but that satellite phone is so unreliable. Perhaps I'll get another battery when the boat calls in to Rupert. Those damn phones are supposed to work just about anywhere. Must be the bloody battery."

"Oh, stop your incessant worrying, Sam. Women have been having babies for centuries. I had no troubles with the first two so why should this one be any different?"

Sam gathered Anna into his arms. "I know, but you said yourself this pregnancy is not like the others. I can't help but worry. Lucky you had home births with Mary and Sara. Still, you had your mom there. Sara knows what to do, but she's so young."

"Sam…give over. I'll be fine, I promise."

◇◇◇◇◇◇◇

Anna clattered the pans as she finished preparing the delayed supper. She had tried to reassure her husband. On the whole, she was satisfied with the compromises that the family had made. She considered them basically self-sufficient.

Her thoughts drifted to the girls. Judging from their attitudes and from the conversations she'd had with both of them, it was evident that they had adapted well to their isolated life.

Mary seemed to feel more secure. The peace and quiet suited her. She didn't have to deal with those who saw her birthmark as a sign of retardation. She was no longer the victim of cruel taunts and beatings from her peers. There were no stares and snickers at the cabin. Here, her family loved and protected her.

Sara appeared to relish the peaceful surroundings, beautiful painting opportunities and following her parent's dream. So far, she gave no indication that she needed companions of her own age. She was able to take correspondence courses that would lead to her arts degree. There was no rush in completing her studies as she hadn't voiced any desire to rejoin the 'real' world any time soon.

Anna called softly. "Is she down yet?"

She heard her daughter get up from the bed. As Sara joined her parents in the main room of their rustic cabin she said, "Yes, she's asleep. Must have been the storm that set her off. Any pie left over from lunch? I'm starving."

While Sara savored the last piece of apple pie, Sam touched his daughter's hand. "You know we are really proud of you, don't you?"

Anna watched as Sara smiled faintly. She wondered if Sara were truly content. Certainly, Sara knew they were proud of her but there seemed to be no end of her responsibility for her sister. What if she did want to go to art school like Grandma had suggested? They couldn't manage without Sara's help unless Mary made some improvement. Mary seemed as though she was plateauing. Anna couldn't see much progress, especially on a night like this.

◇◇◇◇◇◇◇

Sam tossed fitfully in his bunk in the bow of the fish boat. It was the roughest area on the vessel for sleeping, but he valued his privacy. Besides, most of the crew, with the exception of the captain and his first mate, spoke only Korean. Listening to their loud chatter often drove him to seek solitude either here or on the deck.

That deck was out of the question right now. Swells and rollers coming in off the rocks were tossing the boat around like a cork. He thought that the ocean always seemed more treacherous in the fall. However, earnings were better then. Sun Soon-Chun was expert at locating the salmon runs. Right now that money was needed for the new satellite phone to replace the unreliable one at the homestead. Sun Soon-Chun had looked at it and agreed that the only thing to do was to replace it. The captain had a line on a new one but it couldn't be delivered before winter. It would come out with the supplies in the spring. Sam finally gave up trying to sleep and joined the men in the galley where a game of poker was in full swing.

Gesturing that he wanted in on the game, Sam settled down to play. Once the game was started, there was little need for him to be able to speak Korean. These guys knew just enough English to fleece their mechanic.

The Soju flowed freely and the cards were against him. Sam didn't let on to Anna but a good portion of his wages often went to paying off his poker debts. The booze was a problem as well. She could tell he was slipping back into his old drinking habits when he brought back some of the Soju each season. It had caused a few arguments between them.

Thinking of Anna, he wondered how she was doing. She'd looked pretty drawn and tired when he left. She wasn't having an easy time of this pregnancy. He threw in his hand and went to stand in the wheelhouse looking out over the heaving sea. Three more weeks or so and he'd be home.

Chapter 17

KARL SENSED THAT SOMEONE WAS STALKING HIM. OCCASIONALLY he caught brief glimpses of a person dogging his progress through the darkened streets of Anchorage. Quickly rounding a corner, he flattened himself against the rough stucco wall. Willing himself to breathe quietly, he waited.

Footsteps crunched in the loose gravel. Then as if his follower realized that he was making too much racket, the footsteps slowed and became more cautious. They stopped.

From his vantage point, Karl saw a tall figure pause and look around. Karl waited, trying to blend into the shadows cast by the street light. Slowly the figure retraced its steps to the corner. Karl heard the gravel spew sideways as his stalker turned down the alley and passed by him. His arm snaked towards the movement. His bat connected.

Bending over the crumpled form, he shoved hard with his boot. The now upturned, bloodied face gazed blindly towards Karl. Karl searched his memory, but he didn't know the dark-skinned man who lay before him.

As moans issued from between gravelled lips, Karl raised the bat again. "Who the hell are you?" he demanded. "What do you want with me?"

Fear and pain etched themselves in the injured man's eyes, as he scrabbled backwards trying to regain his footing.

Karl pushed the bat down on the man's chest and held it there. "I repeat…what do you want with me, you son of a bitch?"

Muffled sounds crept from the mangled mouth. Coughing and spluttering erupted as the man struggled to respond.

Eventually, Karl was able to hear the words 'George, boss and money'. Connecting the dots, Karl knew that this was a message from the cartel. His days in this town were numbered. He may have won this round, but others would be sure to follow.

Karl brandished his bat over the sprawled legs. "If you don't want to feel this wood smash your legs, you tell George and his so called boss where they can shove their money. I don't have it, anyway. Ren and his mates took it. Beat me and left me for dead in the bush. Tell George that's where the money went. Tell George to shake down Ren. Tell George McKinnon to fuck off."

Quickly he made his way back towards the more brightly lit area of downtown Anchorage. Karl knew he had to split. He'd spent this last year hiding out in small towns in both Canada and the States. The cartel had caught up to him, and he sensed it was just a matter of time before they gained the upper hand. The organization was enormous. Their resources were unlimited.

Crossing through the Chinese section of the city, he rapidly returned to his digs. The rather seedy hotel had been home for less than a month. Now, he was forced to move on, but not before he retrieved what was left of his money.

He carefully felt underneath the heavy dresser drawer. Impatiently, his fingers sought plastic. With a quick jerk, the bread bag fell onto the floor. The thick wad of cash was from the sale of the last of Beth's nuggets. Slowly over the months, he'd taken to cashing them in a bit at a time. He figured that there was no point in drawing attention to oneself. The final nugget, the biggest one, had brought in six hundred plus.

He packed quickly, taking only a couple of changes of clothes and his essentials. With one last look around his tiny room, he punched the taxi cab number into his cellphone. "Need to get to the airport," Karl shouted into the phone. "Plane leaves in forty-five minutes…can you get me there in time for security?"

"It'll be tight, but I'll send the cab right away. Why don't you call the airline and say you're stuck in traffic? This is a small airport. They might hold the plane."

Karl made it with five minutes to spare. Pre-boarding had already taken place by the time he was rushed through security. Settling into the last aisle seat on the plane, he was pleasantly surprised to find the window seat occupied by a woman…a very attractive woman.

"Hi," she said. "You must be someone important. They held the plane for you."

Karl chuckled. "Nah, I just got lucky. Lucky to get the plane and lucky to sit next to you."

She smiled and laughed. "Use that line a lot? I'm off to Vancouver. Where are you heading?"

"Me, I'm going to Mexico for the holidays," Karl lied.

At Vancouver International, he booked on a flight to Peru and went in search of breakfast. He had six hours to kill. It was a nine hour flight with three stops. He was going to need coffee.

◇◇◇◇◇◇◇

Life in Peru was not expensive. Living in the capital city had many advantages. Even in this laid back city, he could find a game when-ever he needed one. In fact, there were three large casinos in the Mira Flores district alone: The Majestic, Fiesta and Atlantic City.

Karl wandered down the back alleys towards the older rundown section of town. He was a regular at the three big casinos but tonight, he needed an infusion of cash. The big three were already starting to get suspicious of his winning streaks. Here in the out-of-the-way rooms, he could use his special decks with ease. Most of the cliental were hardened gamblers who had been banned from the tonier houses. He knew by keeping to himself, dealing cautiously and playing the marks well, he could make a couple of thousand a night. No one ever suspected his inked cards. They had been well worth replacing after Ren's beating. Ren and his cohorts had scarfed his cards as well as most of his money. Beth's nuggets had paid for more than his living expenses.

Now he supported himself solely on the proceeds from the games and the occasional winnings at the tracks. Karl enjoyed both the dirt and the grass tracks at the Hipodroma de Monterrico. He was becoming quite a regular.

"Hey, Franco," he called to a small wiry man leaning against the door jamb of a dingy diner. "Any action you know of?"

"Sure, but it will cost ya."

"Always does. Where is it tonight?" Karl slipped 10 Nuevo Sols into the man's outstretched hand.

"In the back of that garage over on Siesta Street. You know the one?"

With a nod, Karl was off.

Three blocks towards the east, he came to Lucky Auto. Swiftly climbing the narrow stairs, he knocked on the door and waited. After a long time, he knocked again.

"Hey, you looking for someone?" A young girl stood just inside the door. The heavy smell of garlic and spices wafted through the opening.

"Franco sent me. Said there was a little action happening."

"What colour ya got? High stakes. You got what it takes?"

Karl showed the girl the inside of his wallet. *Christ, they sent out a child. He could've been anyone. They're pretty damn stunned. It should be easy pickings here.*

The girl slammed the door shut and Karl waited. He could hear her mouth running as she told someone that the 'gringo' had a bundle. He didn't speak much Spanish, but he could tell she was impressed.

The door opened and the girl beckoned him inside.

Several men were gathered around a kitchen table in a small darkened room. He nodded and sat down to play. In a few hours he'd made enough to finance his next adventure.

◇◇◇◇◇◇

Karl waited eagerly for the guide, for his Machu Picchu trip, to arrive. He had booked through a reputable company well over six months ago. Since he was staying in Lima, he could fit into any schedule. He fairly rubbed his hands together in excitement. In June, the company had called to say everything was a go.

Looking impatiently around for his guide, he watched as a family of Americans huddled together over by the statue in the main part of the hotel lobby. Karl hoisted his backpack to his shoulder and wandered over to the group. "You all waiting on Arco Tours?" he asked pleasantly. "Going to do Machu Picchu?"

The entire family swung as one, towards him. Eyes assessed his clothes and searched his face for signs of authority. "Are you our guide?" The tall thin gentleman asked, stretching out a skeletal hand.

"No, I guess they must be late. Going on Lima time," Karl joked, referring to the laid back ways of this ancient city.

"Well, I wished they'd hurry up. Been waiting for over half an hour now," griped his rather petite wife. She was as thin as her husband but in all other aspects, his total opposite. He was calm, but she gave off an air of high strung stress.

"Hold on a minute. I think I see someone over there by the entry doors." Karl strode purposefully over to a rather harried individual who was scanning the crowd, anxiously trying to find her clients.

"Hi, I'm Karl. You must be looking for us. Arco Tours?"

A look of sheer relief flooded her chubby face. Colour rose in her cheeks as she stammered and stuttered apologies. "Sorry, so sorry. My first day in charge and I couldn't find the right entrance. Traffic out there is a nightmare."

Karl beckoned the Americans over and they all trooped towards the door. The sullen teenager, with lots better things to do, slouched along in her crocs, tripping slightly over the sill.

With the bus already half full, Karl found himself wedged in between the teen and a woman in her fifties. The stench of garlic was overpowering. The woman must have eaten raw cloves in an effort to cure the cough that constantly racked her throat.

Sighing, Karl settled down to what was going to be a very long bus ride. The route from Lima to the staging point wove through the older sections of town. Karl concentrated on breathing through his mouth and watching the bustling city come to life. Jillian, the guide, prattled on and on about the architecture and the history of the ancient city.

The Peruvians valued their history and their family ties. Karl thought of his family ties which of course were now non-existent. Still, his memories swirled as he remembered his hard-hearted father, his wayward mother and his uncle Sven. He'd enjoyed many wonderful times with Sven, hiking and exploring around their old homestead. That was, until Sven wrecked the family by sleeping with Karl's mother.

Filtering through his misty memories, Karl wondered about the old man. Sven must be pretty well off now. The family always had money tucked away, but since his father's death, the bulk of the old estate would have reverted to the remaining brother. Karl had only received the few assets that had been held in the banks and the proceeds from his father's apartment and homestead. Yes, he thought. There must be a bundle of cash somewhere. Probably Sven had it in his mattress waiting for the day he'd never spend it. Cheap old bastard. Karl could spend that money in a flash.

Shrugging off the past, Karl now concentrated on his immediate future. He was going to walk the Inca Trail to Machu Picchu. He grinned as he mentally checked this off his bucket list for South America. Peru was almost done…this trip and then maybe on to Bolivia. Knowing his money was tight, Karl began to scheme. Lima's casinos were getting too hot and the track was not a sure thing. He couldn't influence the nags and as yet, knew no one on the inside. No, he understood his days in Lima were coming to a close. It was time to move on to a more lucrative location.

He stretched his arms over his head as he attempted to walk off the stiffness brought on by the cramped quarters on the bus. Leaving his pack in a heap with others that were lying near the rough wooden table serving as the registration desk, he grabbed a coffee and a rather stale looking ham sandwich from a local street vendor.

The sun was now high in the sky and the queue for registration had slowed to a trickle. Karl edged up to the table and presented his passport and his very best smile. "Long day," he said to an athletic man in his late fifties. "I imagine you'll be glad to get home for lunch."

"Lunch," snorted the official. "I'll be lucky to get dinner. Here's your hotel voucher, our itinerary and the waivers you must sign and present to us before we head out in the morning. Welcome to Arco Tours. "

Karl grinned enthusiastically. "I'm really excited to be here. This is my last adventure in Peru. I've saved Machu Picchu for the end. Off to Bolivia at the end of the month."

"Well, good on you," replied the Arco representative. "If you enjoy this tour, check out our Bolivian Wildlife and Rainforest Adventure. We offer alumni twenty percent off any future tour."

Karl nodded and collected his backpack. He could see some of the others in the group heading towards the hotel that was their pit stop for the night. Judging by the headache beginning to crowd his temples, he knew an early night was in order.

He groped in his pocket for the altitude sickness meds he'd hoped he wouldn't need. He bought two large bottles of water at the front desk. The price was steep, but Karl was smart in the ways of travelling. His headache probably stemmed from dehydration. Once again he thought of Sven. His uncle had taught him most of his survival skills.

As luck would have it, the next morning he discovered that his place in line, along the narrow path leading to the suspension bridge, was yet again between the sullen teen and madam garlic breath. He hurried along overtaking the teen just past the bridge. "Excuse me, need to talk to the guide."

Once safely past the negative vibes and the pungent odours, Karl slowed his pace and began to relish the physical toil that the trail and altitude were beginning to exert on his body. All his life he'd been fit and apart from his drinking, he was in excellent shape. Breathing deeply, he crested the incline and took in one of the many views that would astound him.

Later that night, after chowing down on a succulent goat stew, Karl lay in his miniscule tent reviewing his current situation. Peru was coming to a close and he needed to decide where to go next. It seemed to have been ages since he had been in Canada. In fact, he needed to touch Canadian soil and renew his passport. Soon to expire, it was easier to get it reissued in Vancouver than to try to go through an embassy in South America. Vancouver presented some problems as far as the cartel was concerned. He wondered if George and the gang had given up on him. Three years was a long time to have been away. For all they knew he was dead.

Punching down his folded up sweatshirt that served as a pillow, Karl turned on his side. He could feel the rough ground through his thin sleeping mat. The tour company provided good meals, but the camping equipment left a lot to be desired. He guessed they counted on their clients being too exhausted to care.

◇◇◇◇◇◇

Landing at Vancouver International later that month, Karl put the next part of his plan in motion. He asked the taxi driver to take him to the little bar that had served those great burgers so many years ago. There was very little chance that George would be there. If he was, Karl would leave quickly before he was noticed.

Shrugging off unpleasant memories of his last trip in a Beaver, Karl inquired at the bar if anyone was heading out to Rupert that day or the next.

"Sure thing," a gravelly voice said from a dimly lit table in the corner of the pub.

Karl turned to see old 'Grizzly Adams', the same old codger who had held court years ago when he had come in here with George. Laughing, he held out two fingers to the bartender. "Two of whatever he's drinking".

Settling into the chair opposite "Grizzly Adams', Karl chuckled. "Where'd your entourage disappeared to?"

"Who? You mean those hangers on? Got fed up with them not believing me stories. Jealous buggers is what they is. Jealous. I can fly the pants off of them fellas any day."

Karl's eyes followed the line of spit the cowboy pilot ejected into a greasy spittoon. "You still fly?"

"Sure as hell do. Still got me license and a plane sitting at the municipal. Pretty little Cessna I got from Stan's widow. She got no use for it now."

"Cessna…hate those bloody Beavers. Say, can you take me to Rupert tomorrow? I can make it worth your while if you keep it under wraps."

Grizz's eyes twinkled and he slapped a big hairy hand on the grimy table. He hawked another one. "You running?"

"Nah, just don't want anyone to see my comings and goings if you know what I mean."

The deal was set and Karl found himself at the municipal airport, the next day, waiting for his ancient pilot. He saw a spry figure in light blue coveralls mosey over to a lone Cessna set apart from the other craft lining the field.

Soon, the man beckoned to Karl. "Don't take all day. Git yer ass over here."

"Christ, I didn't recognize you. You clean up good." There was no trace of the worn out bull shitter from the diner. In his place was a freshly shaven man that looked to be sixty at the most. Yes, Grizz cleaned up good.

Karl felt his gut unclench as the wheels touched down in the smoothest landing he'd ever experienced. After grabbing his stuff and thanking Grizz, Karl made his way into the small hanger that functioned as the terminal on the outskirts of town.

Thankfully, the old pilot had asked no questions when Karl said he needed to land away from the main airport. Karl knew George might be anywhere in Rupert. Not wanting to risk being seen, Karl walked the six kilometres to town.

Knowing that George and crew were not expecting him and that they definitely would not be looking for him in the most expensive hotel in town, Karl checked into the Grand under the name, Bob Hoburg.

He began searching the buy and sell papers for a twenty-eight foot cabin cruiser that would be safe enough for the waters between here and Sven's place. Sure enough, there were several ranging in price from $19,000 for a 1986 Freedom Cabin Cruiser to a boat closer to his limited budget. The Fiberform Executive cruiser was ancient, thirty odd years old, but the price was right. It was listed at $5,600.

◇◇◇◇◇◇

As they chatted, Karl learned that Fredrick, an anemic looking accountant, was eager to deal on his folly. Apparently, his impulsive buy seven years ago was a sore point between his wife and himself. Now that the couple was looking for a down payment to put on a condo on Fleet Street, he needed cash.

"Not sure how well the motor runs," Fredrick said as they looked over the boat in the early morning. "Haven't had it out in the last year. I've kept it covered though."

Karl shrugged. "Since you haven't fired it in a year, it probably needs overhauling. That will cost quite a bit. Mind you, I'm pretty good with engines. Could I do the work here at the dock?"

"Don't see why not. Moorage is paid until the end of the summer."

Karl glanced around. He was pretty satisfied with the out-of-the-way moorage. The boat was tied up close to the end of a finger jutting from the main dock. If he kept his head down and worked early morning or later in the evening when the casinos were in full swing, there was very little chance of running into anyone who might recognize him. He needed tools, though. "You got any tools I could borrow?" he asked Frederick. "Mine are in storage down on the lower mainland."

"Nope. I usually borrowed what I needed from Joe at the marina. He'd probably loan you some for a case of beer. Good guy that one."

They took the boat for another cruise.

"Pretty good for a '79. Still with the amount of work to be done, I couldn't justify offering more than $4,500."

"Wait a minute, that's pretty thin. Have to get at least $5,000. It's hardly been used since I've had it. Didn't have much history before that either. You get the moorage until September as well, don't forget."

They dickered around for a while and settled on what both considered a fair price. The accountant was happy to finally get rid of his boat and Karl was happy to have a bargain.

◇◇◇◇◇◇

"Hey, Joe," Karl called to a bent over back belonging to a fisherman scraping out some smelly containers. "Fredrick told me you might loan me a few tools. I just bought that old Fiberform from him."

"Shit, someone finally bought that rust bucket. Well, I'll be damned. He's been looking to unload that ever since he and Beverly set up housekeeping."

Joe took a long look at Karl. "You know he didn't use it much. Must be well over a year since he's had those engines running."

"I turned both over yesterday. Volvo made good V8s back then. They run rough but they did start. Figure I'll replace all the fluids and do some tinkering. My uncle showed me a lot about engines. Mostly Mercs, but an engine is an engine."

"Yeah, Volvos are pretty sweet. If you have any troubles give me a holler. Have a look in that tool chest…just be sure to bring everything back, now." Joe turned and picked up his scrub brush again.

As Joe cleaned his pails, Karl scrutinized the extraordinarily tidy tool kit. Selecting what he needed, he waved and sauntered up the sloping dock. The slant was increasing as the tide went out. His calf muscles were giving him the gears ever since he'd climbed Machu Picchu. He knew he must get on to trying those stretching exercises that the cute little massage therapist told him about. He snickered to himself. He'd shown her, a few exercises and then some.

A week and a half, three cases of Canadian, and several pieces of Joe's advice resulted in two very smooth running engines. They positively purred.

As he tested his boat in the bay, he gained even more confidence in it. The turning ability was good. It tracked true. The wheelhouse was tight and managed to keep out the incessant rain that fell like clockwork, on this coast.

Karl realized that he'd gotten himself a pretty decent boat for five thousand plus some hard graft.

CHAPTER 18

ANNA FELT AS THOUGH THE DAYS WERE DRAGGING LIKE THE SNAIL trailing down the sides of the water barrel. She rubbed her swollen belly and wished for relief. Since her cycles had never been regular, it was difficult to tell when this baby would make its appearance. Both she and Sam were praying it would come before the Koreans came to get him for spring fishing. Sure, the girls knew what to do, but she wanted her husband beside her. He'd been there for the other births and she was afraid this was going to be the exception. The baby had not dropped and still rode high just below her breastbone. Unable to eat very much, Anna was becoming more and more tired as the pregnancy wore on. Sleeping was impossible as this baby continually kicked and punched.

Tearfully, she turned to Sam as they lay in their bed that night. "I wish this was over already. I'm so tired of it all. I swear, Sam, this is the last baby. No more after this."

Sam patted her shoulder. "Here, turn over. I'll give you one of my famous back rubs."

Anna turned slowly like a lumbering elephant. Every part of her body ached. Oh, how she wished this was all over.

With Sam rubbing her back, Anna soon began to relax.

"I don't think junior is coming before I have to leave." Sam said, his voice betraying his fears. "Tomorrow I'm going to take the run-about over to Thoresen Island and make contact with the old man. I'd feel better if you could get help if you needed it."

"I don't think you should bother. Remember how Sun Soon-Chun said the old guy threatened him with a shotgun when they tried to tie up to his dock. What makes you think he wants to be disturbed by you?"

"Well, maybe he just doesn't like foreigners. It won't take me more than an hour or so to get over there." Sam drew his wife closer and settled into sleep.

◇◇◇◇◇◇

The next morning, Sam cast off, gunned the motor and headed out across the bay and into the narrow strait that separated the two homesteads. As he jarred his way through the cresting waves, he wondered about the reception he might get. It wasn't long before he found out.

The click of a shotgun bolt, as it slammed into place, was his first clue.

"I don't know you. Shove off my dock."

Sam was peering down the wrong end of a shotgun. A doddery old man shook as he pointed the weapon at Sam's head.

"Hey, Mr. Thoresen, I just wanted to make your acquaintance. I'd have been over sooner, but I heard you don't like visitors. Heard that you prefer to be on your own. The wife and I bought your brother's place a few years back. I could do with a bit of your help."

"Don't give a damn who you say you are. I said, shove off my deck." The unkempt hermit started muttering and swearing as he brandished his gun.

Sam, fearing that the hermit might either accidentally or delib-erately shoot him, leaned out of the boat and shoved the spare oar into the crumbling wood. Turning to the outboard motor, he yanked the starter cord. Thankfully, the motor roared into life.

"You were right about the old man. I want none of you to ever go near that island. The guy has gone bush. He's crazier than a loon. Nuttier than a fruit cake. Whatever, just don't venture over there for any reason. I was scared he was going to pop me."

"Don't worry, Sam. We'll have no need to bother old man Thoresen. The baby will come before you leave. Everything will be all right. You'll see."

The Coast Guard came by a week later. Anna greeted them with glee. Steven and his new partner Jennifer had brought two letters, one from her mother and one from a dear friend. Buoyed up by the letters, Anna bustled about getting supper for her guests. Since they rarely had visitors, she dragged out her seldom used china and set a fine table. She was delighted to meet Jennifer. The officer seemed close to her own age.

As everyone gathered around the plank table, Sam started passing the dishes of food.

"When are you due, Mrs. Lindholm?" Jennifer asked. "If you don't mind me saying so, it looks like any day now."

Anna laughed. 'Oh, call me Anna, please. I'm really not sure. I'm hoping for sooner, not later. Maybe tonight while you're here."

"Well, we're going to keep an eye on your increasing family, Sam. You have our call number if you need us. Do you have a radio or and a satellite phone?"

"Sure do, except neither works very well right now," Sam answered quickly. "Think the satellite's battery is faulty. I'll get another if we call into anywhere that has shopping."

"Speaking of shopping; would you mind picking up a few things, for us? I forgot to order enough flour and need a few other things as well. Nothing that can't wait to be delivered on your next pass. The Koreans usually bring our stuff in the fall, but I screwed up big time with the flour. Blame it on, junior," Anna said ruefully. "I don't know where my mind is half the time."

"Sure thing," Steven assured her. "We've got room to store some flour in the cabin. Can't have it getting wet, now can we?"

"I'm so impressed by your self-sufficient home. I wish I were adventurous enough to live in isolation, but I'd be too lonely," Jennifer said wistfully. "You're so courageous to have a baby with just your family's support. No doctor, no neighbours…"

"People have been birthing babies alone since the beginning of time. I had the first two just fine. They were home births."

◇◇◇◇◇◇

Anna was wrong about two things. The baby didn't come that night and the baby didn't come before Sam left to fish. The Koreans came for Sam two days later.

Waving goodbye as the Korean vessel set off out the bay, she was gripped by panic.

Mary shot an anxious glance at Sara. "Mom's worried. I can tell."

Sara put her arm around her sister's shoulders. "Don't worry. We both know what to do. Didn't we watch Daisy, our goat, have her kid last year? Besides Dad wouldn't have left if he didn't think we could handle it. We are true pioneers now. Tilling the land and birthing babies." She tried to make light of their situation, but she felt more than a little apprehensive. She hoped nothing would go wrong. There would be no time to get help even if the temperamental satellite phone decided to work.

Over the next two weeks, there was very little free time to spend worrying. An exhausted Anna spent most of her time slouched in her rocker giving the girls their orders. Sara and Mary did their best to appease the cranky expectant mother. Once in a while, Anna would praise their efforts, but mostly she dozed on and off immersed in her own world.

CHAPTER 19

MARY FELT A WARM SENSE OF PRIDE WHENEVER SHE THOUGHT about Samuel's birth. It surprised her that although she'd been scared, she had been okay. Maybe it was because she had to be strong. The pain and suffering wasn't happening to her; it was happening to someone she loved desperately.

As Anna had stifled her moans and struggled with contractions, she and Sara had done whatever was necessary. Throughout the long night, they had remained strong, united in their task. Eventually, her precious baby brother made his squalling entrance into this world.

Anna slowly collected herself and went over to the bucket of warmed water. She stripped and washed every part of her spent body. Then taking her screaming infant from Sara, she sat down heavily in her rocking chair. Barely able to keep her eyes open, she began to nurse her son.

Mary had never seen so much blood and mess. It took the girls a long time to clean up while Anna sat feeding the newborn. They bundled up the blood soaked sheets and chucked them out of the cabin door. After that, they sponged down the mattress as best they could and flipped it over.

Anna staggered over to the freshly made bed and lay down with her son clutched in her arms. She managed to smile at her girls. "I'm so proud of you, two. Samuel had two angels to help him into this world. Thank you..." She was asleep before she could finish her sentence.

Sara gently moved Samuel out of Anna's arms and laid him away from his mother.

It was hardly necessary as Anna wouldn't move or wake for hours. Only the cries of her son managed to rouse her from the deepest sleep of her life.

Mary nodded with satisfaction as she remembered how well she and Sara had coped. It amazed her that she hadn't retreated to that dark place in her mind. Maybe the demons were leaving. Perhaps the happiness that Samuel brought with him was enough to drive them away. Perhaps.

◇◇◇◇◇◇

Sara and Mary eagerly scrambled up the cliff path. They had a precious hour to go exploring while Anna and Samuel napped in the cool cabin. The chores were done for now and the afternoon beckoned. They climbed eagerly, relishing the warmth of the sun and the gentle breeze.

Frantically Mary grabbed at roots, rocks, grasses— anything as she slid rapidly towards the edge of the cliff. Her ankle twisted painfully underneath her slithering body. She came to a bruising stop against a huge boulder. She held onto the rock with everything she had. Dust rose up, choking her as she tried to regain her sense of balance.

"Sara, Sara," she gasped as terror swept over her. She was staring into a hidden crevasse. Its rough, narrow sides led straight down to the ocean below. The crevasse was at least fifty feet, maybe more, deep. Cool moist air, mixed with odours of rotting kelp, swept over her as the waves eddied in and out of the narrow chasm. Spray lashed at the rocks. The waves swirled relentlessly.

"Hang on, Mary. Hold tight." Sara reached her sister and dragged her to safety. After regaining their wits, the girls lay down flat on their stomachs and inched towards the edge. They both peered over, staring into the churning channel. Waves crashed and resonated in the cavernous fissure. Spray reached nearly halfway to the top of the crevasse. As the water receded, they caught sight of a deer carcass wedged firmly near the bottom. Most of the body was simply bones. It had been devoured by crabs.

"Good God, Mary that could've been you." Sara shuddered at the thought. "Let's not tell Mom and Dad what happened. We'll just say we found a crevasse. Have to warn them. It's hard to see, just like the cave. You don't see it before you are there."

Together they piled some rocks on top of each other to resemble an Inuit inukshuk and then after retracing their steps carefully; finished climbing up the path. The view from the top of the cliff seemed especially wonderful after such a close call.

◇◇◇◇◇◇

After the days had lengthened and spring had eased into summer, Sam returned. He was simply delighted with his son and so very proud of all his girls. Sara and Mary seemed to have everything in hand. They had managed the birth and now appeared to do most of the chores around the cabin and garden. He could tell that the pregnancy had taken its toll on Anna. Concerned, he told her to take things slowly. "The girls and I can finish planting the garden. You just look after my son."

Gradually he saw colour brighten his wife's face and strength return to her body. Samuel still slept in their room, but he could tell Anna was starting to long for his love making. He rejoiced at his good fortune. Here he was in paradise, away from the horrors of city life. He had a beautiful wife and three wonderful children. Soon the garden would be ready for harvesting and fall would be coming. Then he sighed as he thought of the approaching fishing season. Wishing he didn't have to leave again so soon, he put away his hoe and entered the cabin's cool sanctuary.

"Party time, girls," he called as he came through the doorway. "I'm going to finish chopping the last of the deadfall. You get to plan our celebration."

Two hours later, whole wheat lasagna was slowly baking in the oven. Some of Anna's just baked bread had been slathered in goat butter and wild garlic. Mary had made some chocolate pudding and Sara had finished setting the table with all the fanciest dishes she could find.

Anna was washing garden fresh lettuce in the kitchen bucket. "Here, will you empty this out over the cucumber plants, please?" she asked Mary.

Mary, always anxious to please, rushed to complete the task almost tripping over her father as he came back in from chopping wood.

"Oops," he laughed. "What's the hurry? Not like we're late for class." He smiled at his daughter. He thought she seemed much better lately. She gave no indication that she was still worried about her looks. No one really noticed any more. Her long, wild hair often fell over that side of her face and with her healthy tan, the ugly birthmark had lost much of its starkness. Samuel had indeed been a Godsend. Mary completely doted on her brother. If Anna wasn't holding him, Mary was.

Sure, he allowed, she still grew silent whenever they had visitors. She would fidget and squirm until her nerves got the better of her. Then she'd make a dash for the cave. Visitors were pretty rare, so he really didn't worry too much about it. He understood that as time passed, there was a good chance of her outgrowing some of her fears. Once again, he cursed the likes of Sharon and her gang.

◇◇◇◇◇◇

August 21st the Koreans came to pick up Sam again. Sara carefully wrote the date in her leather bound notebook. She kept a diary of all the events that shaped their world. Most of the entries were quite mundane, but her artistic nature showed throughout her scribbling. Alongside her logs, she often drew small sketches. Sometimes, she used whole pages for a quick drawing that would one day become either a watercolour or an oil painting.

This time, Captain Sun Soon-Chun had remembered to bring her painting supplies. She hugged the shy man causing him to blush profusely. Happily spreading out her new-found treasures, she gazed at the bounty. A huge stack of canvases, several sketch blocks and best of all both water and oil paints lay scattered across the wooden table.

Anna gently reminded her that the table was needed since she was about to serve tea to their guests.

Humming happily to herself, Sara lovingly collected her bonanza and carted it off to her room. Once more she thanked Sun Soon-Chun for bringing her supplies.

◇◇◇◇◇◇◇

Parting was usually difficult, but Sam could hardly bear leaving this time. He stood for a long while at the railing, watching as his family disappeared from view. Rubbing his hands over his weathered face, he turned and joined the crew in the wheelhouse. "Might be my last trip," he said to the captain. "I hate to leave them on their own like this. Don't know how I'd make ends meet though. Just can't grow enough wheat to last the winter. Always need money for one thing or another."

Sam knew Sun Soon-Chun understood. He appreciated that the captain felt the tug of his own family. Sun Soon-Chun's wife and child remained in Rupert while he fished. The captain was used to this hard life and understood that this was his lot. He was a fisherman. He and his crew had shares in the boat and after each catch was sold, the cash was divided amongst themselves according to their stake. It worked out, but the captain was one of the first to admit that none of them were rich. They barely made a living.

The Korean said sympathetically, "I know it is hard to leave. We need you on the boat. No one can fix the problems like you can. Come let's look at that fuel line. Engine choked quite a bit coming into your bay. Could be dirty fuel; could be fouled line. Come on, we need to look now before we get too far out in the strait." With that the captain smiled ruefully at his friend and led the way to the stern.

CHAPTER 20

SWEAT DRIPPED DOWN HER BACK AND GATHERED UNDER THE brim of her hat that shielded her from a merciless sun. Wiping her forehead with the hem of her dress, Anna glanced around feeling the oppressive forest closing in. Sharp prickly thorns from ever-present thistles raked at her calloused hands as she bent to her task, grasping and pulling, trying to eradicate the stubborn weeds. Dirt encrusted her hands, caking under the nails like inky black mold.

Crossing over to the tool shed, she lifted a wooden lid and thrust an old tin cup into the water barrel. The barrel was always full, since it was gravity fed from a creek further up in the woods. Gulping down the cool liquid, she felt her parched throat ease. Carelessly, she refilled the dipper and poured water directly down her front, soaking her dress. She shivered delightedly at its shocking coldness.

With renewed energy, she grabbed a rusty hoe and hacked furiously at the tough roots. Its dull edge crushed the stems. Damp earth smells mixed with bitter odours from plant juices and rose up to meet the still, humid air. Wasps struggled to dig deeper into the vegetation; swirling angrily as the hoe disturbed their quest for moisture.

Straightening up, she wearily arched her back to release the gathering tension. Suddenly swaying in the overwhelming heat, she sat down heavily on a nearby stump. From her seat, Anna once again carefully surveyed the woods in an attempt to conquer the claustrophobic atmosphere that threatened to send her running to the cabin.

If she let her imagination run freely, she could see eyes peering from the bushes and hear the haunting cry of Windego, the wild woman of the woods. The feeling was always worse in the heavy heat of summer. In the stifling air, the forest seemed to beckon with fingers of the damp squishy moss that covered every surface. The rainforest pulled at her with the promise of coolness and respite from the burning rays of the noon sun. The sinister promise, that her cares would disappear if she succumbed to the lure of the woods, fascinated Anna. She would be smothered by soft, bottomless green while vines and old man's beard held her down. Sometimes the attraction was just too great and she'd have to dash for the safety of the cabin.

Thankfully, she heard the cries of Samuel waking from his nap. Unlike his sister, Mary, who had suffered from colic, he was an easy baby. The even-tempered infant slept well.

"Sara and Mary, come pull the weeds from around the carrots for me. Sam's awake and needs to be fed."

◇◇◇◇◇◇

Sara raised her head from the book she was busy reading. She had been engrossed in one of her father's 'back-to-the-land' books. This one dealt with raising pigs on a small acreage. *Take care that the pens are large enough to ensure the piglets are not crushed by the sow. Barriers can be set up to protect the litter from being rolled on.* It was a useless book for this patch of wilderness; considering that this cabin was set in the middle of a clearing scarcely two acres in size. Still, if they were able to bring in a boar and a couple young sows, they might be able to raise enough pork for their own needs. None of them really enjoyed hunting the small deer that roamed the forest.

Then there was always the problem of feed. The goats managed on garden leftovers and grain they ordered from Rupert. Goats were pretty good scroungers as well. They managed to fill their bellies wherever they wandered. Allowed to roam freely during the day, the goats were shut in at night. A couple of shakes of the grain bucket and they usually came running.

She had to concede, pigs were much more high maintenance. Still, it was a possibility and she planned on talking things over with her father. Now, that she was close to nineteen, he listened to her suggestions and often included her in the major decisions around the homestead.

They had tried to increase the actual farming area by removing some logs, stumps and trees but were only successful in reclaiming a small amount of land. Next, they had attempted to increase the land's fertility by digging kelp, food wastes and fish scraps into the garden plot. It was difficult to provide the goats with enough grazing. The herd was steadily increasing so they would be even more dependent on the supplemental grain. Unfortunately, the cost of feed was always going up. They had hopes of clearing more land next spring.

Although she often wondered about her father's ways, Sara was amazed that they had done as well as they had. He was consumed with the idea of living off the grid and becoming self-sufficient.

This homestead was proving to be a difficult location for farming. Soil here was shallow and the temperate rainforest was only suitable for the very hardiest of crops. Root vegetables did the best. Small patches of wheat hardly grew tall enough to cut. She grimaced as she thought of all the effort it took to harvest even a pound of grain. Still, if she understood her father as well as she thought she did, she knew his days of fishing were quickly coming to an end. He hated leaving his family alone. Now that Samuel had arrived, she could tell that it was ripping him apart to work for the Koreans. Her heart ached as she remembered him leaning over the railing with his anguished face, half hidden in his hands. She had watched and waved until the vessel became a mere dot on the horizon.

Sighing, she closed the book on raising pigs. There were lots of books in his collection, but most of them were about raising vegetables, chickens, fishing or surviving on next to nothing. There was hardly an adventure book among them.

Sara missed her previous life in the city that had been complete with friends, school, noise and books. She missed swimming in the recreation centre pool. Occasionally, she screwed up enough courage to plunge into the ocean but it was always too cold. Aside from the pool, the center had also offered art activities during the holidays. Sometimes she felt that here, her art was suffering. There was no one to criticize her efforts. The family always raved about her work but were they just being kind? She longed for some kind of criticism.

Sara was thankful her painting supplies had been renewed at last. Over the winter her paints had dwindled down to next to nothing. Now, she was running out of paper. She held out hope that her dad would remember to bring her some from the Mainland.

Sara listened. If it weren't for the constant seething and crashing of the sea against the rocky shore, it would be as quiet as a tomb here. However, following the example set by her father; Sara poured her energies into this new way of life. She rarely complained.

"Come on," she said to her younger sister. "Best we hop to it. You know how grouchy Mum can get in this heat." She went to retrieve her hat, gardening gloves and the chicken bucket for the weeds.

"Okay, I'll just get my hat. I got a headache, yesterday. Too much sun. Thank God the potatoes are done. Can't stand the banana slugs that hang out there," Mary answered.

Sara loved her younger sister dearly and they usually did everything together. Mom was always looking after Samuel and seemed to have little time for them anymore. Sara treated her sister as an equal, always patiently explaining things and showing her what needed to be done.

She agreed with Mary. Babies did take a lot of looking after, however, she had noticed her mum was becoming more and more withdrawn since Samuel's birth. Samuel meant everything to her mother. It was as if this new life was in need of protection and must be treasured or it would be lost. The only time she seemed truly happy and at ease was when she was nursing or holding the baby. Anna could spend hours playing with, rocking and soothing her son.

◇◇◇◇◇◇

Anna reached into the homemade crib and lifted out her son. Little Samuel filled her life with joy. He was the only thing that kept her going in this God-forsaken wilderness. Certainly she loved her girls and they were company, but the girls had each other. Samuel was hers and hers alone. His father, Sam, didn't come into the equation. Baby Samuel hardly knew his namesake.

Samuel had been born while he was away fishing for those Koreans. Following her instructions, gasped between contractions, Mary and Sara had managed the birth. The event had gone smoothly; she was loathed to think what might have happened if something had gone wrong. There was a lot to be said for the sterile expertise of modern medicine. Once again, she cursed the wilderness and isolation that came with being married to Sam.

As she changed little Samuel's cloth diaper, Anna tickled his tummy with her soft brown hair, relishing in his sweet baby smell. His eyes lit up as he laughed and kicked his feet. Then sitting in her grandmother's rocker, she fed her son, smiling at his fist clutching her breast while he pulled eagerly on the nipple. For the first time that day she was at peace. She could forget the beckoning woods, her absent husband and all the worries of her wilderness life. "Come on, little man. Let's settle you on the porch in the sun while I get to that bread."

Giving him one of Mary's old rag dolls to play with, she left him on the deck surrounded by two old cushions and a couple of cardboard boxes that held firewood. He was too young to crawl, but she wanted to be sure he wouldn't roll anywhere. His motor skills were right on track. He was beginning to do that funny rocking on his belly which often led to crawling. Both girls had walked early and she was sure that Samuel would follow suit.

Samuel cooed as he smacked the doll against the faded boards. His little arms were rising and falling in the sunbeams. His sparse hair stood straight up mimicking a halo in the sun.

After sprinkling whole wheat flour over the smooth wooden counter, she reached into the bowl of raised dough, scooping it out onto the satiny wood. She began kneading the pliant dough. As yeast smells tickled her nose, she hummed. Her hands sank into the warm dough, lifting, turning and pushing as she fell into a rhythm. This was one chore she loved. Although she had taught Sara how to make bread, she seldom gave up this old fashioned pleasure.

As she watched Samuel from the kitchen window, her thoughts once again turned to her absent husband. Sam was a handsome man with abundant charm. They had met at a church social and had fallen in love quickly. They married as soon as they realized Sara was on the way. She sometimes wondered if she would have been so eager to marry if she'd known what the future would bring.

Sam was a man with a mission. In this time of hurry and waste, he wanted to carve out his own space in the natural world. He wanted time to pass slowly, to savour his family and to be self-sufficient, beholden to no one.

Anna sighed deeply. Yes, she wanted to support his dream of wilderness living, but he wasn't the one left to cope with three children in the bush. Every fishing season he got to leave and work away for periods of time. They needed the cash he would earn for things they couldn't produce like flour, sugar, salt, cloth, medicines and of course, his whiskey.

Lately, he'd taken to drinking that Soju. She fervently hoped he wasn't slipping back into his old dependency. The last time he'd given in to the booze, she had nearly packed her bags. There was no question of doing that now. Both of them were too heavily invested in this project to ever leave. Whatever the future brought; this was home.

He had been gone for three months. She was lonely and longed for adult company. She yearned for the feeling of her husband's arms around her, holding her as they lay listening to the wind moan and the sea churn the rocks on the beach. Turning to each other on such nights, they could make time stand still. She loved him. It was as simple as that.

There were no neighbors for miles except for old man Thoresen. His homestead and theirs was separated by over five miles of rough water. They never saw the old man venture from his remote island. He was supposed to be nearly ninety.

Their land had been owned by the old man's brother. Since they had dealt with a real estate agent, the previous owner's family was a mystery to them. Apart from meeting him when the papers were signed, they knew nothing about the owner's son, Thoresen's nephew. Rumors had it that the old man had no other family. Judging from the reception Sam had received when he tried to make contact, the old guy actively discouraged visitors of any kind. He lived alone in his dilapidated shack and would probably die alone with no one to mourn him.

Shaking her head, she tried to think of more pleasant things. Tonight they would have venison with a hodgepodge of new potatoes, baby carrots and peas for supper. There was a bit of Barney Goose left over for dessert. If Daisy, the milk goat, had dropped her kid they would have had cream, but she was late this time. Billy, their male goat, was agitated so she might be getting close. She should check Daisy's udder tonight for signs of a coming birth.

Punching down the dough, she began to shape the loaves. Metal loaf pans were lined up like coffins on the stove waiting to be filled. Lift, turn, and roll.

She sensed rather than saw the tawny blur pass by the broken windowpane. She felt a soft thud shake the deck. Anna looked up from the floured surface to see Samuel hanging limply in the big cat's jaws. Her baby's legs swung lazily as the cougar slowly turned and gazed straight at Anna. The cat's amber eyes glinted in the brilliant sunshine. With slow, easy movements, it jumped down into the garden; loping off into the foreboding forest as silently as it had appeared.

Her gut rippled. Grabbing her belly in horror, she screamed to the girls. "A cougar! My God! A cougar! Get inside quick! Get inside!"

Snatching up a butcher knife, Anna thrust her feet into her rubber boots and was out the door and down the steps.

Sara and Mary stared at the image of their mother stumbling into the undergrowth, her boots hindering her progress and desperation blinding her to the branches whipping at her head. Shocked into action, they fled to the cabin, reaching the door just as Anna's faded blue housedress vanished from view.

◇◇◇◇◇◇

Time passed in halting drips. The wind picked up and branches began to creak in the treetops. As darkness stole over the cabin, both girls began to sob. Their mother had been gone far too long. In the evening's growing chill, the small wooden home cooled quickly.

Too distraught to go to bed, the girls lit a small fire in the wood stove and huddled down beside it, wrapping themselves up in an old quilt from Anna's bed. Clinging to each other, they faced the endless night ahead.

"Shh," Sara said attempting to soothe her younger sister. "It's too dark out. She's got no light with her. She is probably waiting until morning to make her way home. Shh, try to sleep for a bit."

Eventually they both fell into an uneasy sleep only to waken at first light. Usually, Anna would have lit the stove and coffee would be percolating on the top. No smell of brewing coffee and no warmth greeted the girls.

"We have to go look for her," Mary said curling down further into the warm quilt. "She's been gone too long. What if she's hurt or lost?"

"I don't want to go in the forest with that cougar lurking around. Besides, Mom told us to stay inside," Sara said sternly.

She rose swiftly and relit the fire in the stove. Moving quickly, she boiled some porridge, added a spoonful of maple syrup and set a bowl of the lumpy mixture in front of Mary. "Eat up. We'll need energy if we are going to go after mum," she said.

Mary gave Sara a grateful look and began spooning the chunky mush into her mouth. "Mom's probably pretty hungry too," Mary whispered.

Dawn came and went, leaving the harsh brilliance of the summer sun beating down on the clearing around the cabin. They dressed in jeans and long sleeved shirts to protect themselves from the prickly brush and biting insects. The girls pulled on their rubber boots and started into the woods holding tightly to each other's hands.

Making their way along a faint animal trail, they pushed on scarcely noticing branches scratching at their limbs and snatching at their hair. Moisture from the fallen nursery logs and ever present moss dampened their clothes and chilled their bare feet enclosed in the loose rubber footwear. They released their hands in order to crawl over the fallen trees and rocks that blocked the path. Terrified, they constantly scanned the brush for the cougar. Desperation drove them further into the dense woods. Ever mindful of the path's direction and the moss growing on the north side of the trees, they walked and shouted.

"Mom, Mom. Where are you, Mommy? Can you hear us? Mom, Mom." Their voices were quickly swallowed by the unforgiving rainforest. Moving at a snail's pace, they pushed on in vain hope.

"Oh, God, no!" Sara stood shock still. "Mary, look."

Hidden, half covered in the forest litter lay what was left of Anna clutching Samuel in her arms.

Slowly, Sara approached the bodies. Flies swarmed up from the dried blood. The stench of death and cat was overwhelming. Stillness echoed and all hope vanished as she stared down at the faded blue dress. "Mommy," she whispered. "Mommy!"

Mary heaved and retched. She wiped her mouth with the back of her hand, staring at the dreadful sight. Her mother and little Samuel were gone. Only a pile of flesh and clothing had been left behind. Flies buzzed about the blood soaked remains. She shook and retched again, gasping for air. "What are we going to do? We can't leave them here," whimpered Mary scanning the shadows for movement.

Shoving Samuel up under the bloody housedress, they tied the baby to Anna's chest with Anna's apron strings. The girls took off their shirts and knotted the sleeves together. Roping the shirts under Anna's armpits, they hauled their burden along the deer trail. Slowly and hideously, they struggled back to the cabin dragging the bodies with them.

◇◇◇◇◇◇◇

Weeping in frustration, they took turns trying to pound the old manure shovel into the hard ground beside the chicken coop. The top layer of soil had quickly given way to impenetrable rock. The soil was too thin there. The girls knew that the garden soil was deeper, especially after they had added kelp and compost this spring, but neither wanted to bury the bodies there. They soon realized that it was impossible to dig a deep enough hole to protect Anna and Samuel from scavengers. "We can't do this. We just can't," moaned Mary stabbing at the hard surface.

"I know, I know. But we can't leave them. If we do, the cougar will be back for sure," stated Sara.

"What did the natives do with their dead?" asked Mary.

"Probably put them in a tree or cave…I don't know," Sara snapped.

Sara examined the clearing. The cabin, goat shed, tool shed, garden and small patch of grazing land seemed to mock her. She gave up trying for a proper solution to the problem. "Help me get them into the tool shed. Dad will know what to do when he gets back," ordered Sara.

"At least, there they'll be safe from the cougar and the rain," Mary agreed.

Hauling the tools and farm implements out of the tool shed, they piled the equipment under the porch. The girls managed to wedge the bodies into the small shed. Then they boarded up the door with planks and nails.

Mary ran into the cabin and returned a short while later. In her hands she had a piece of cardboard. Sobbing softly, she nailed it to the shed door. *Mommy and baby Samuel we love you* was printed in careful schoolgirl letters.

Exhausted, they spent another night cuddled up together in front of the wood stove wrapped in Anna's quilt.

Early the next day, they walked to the point. Hoping against hope, they stared out to sea fervently wishing to spot the Korean boat on the horizon. Nothing moved except the seagulls constantly whirling above the distant islands. The horizon remained empty and the sun rose higher in the sky. The glare hurt their eyes as they searched the open sea.

"Maybe he'll come tonight," Mary said in a faint voice.

Reaching for her sister's hand Sara replied, "Don't worry, he'll come soon. He has to."

"We'll just have to keep real busy. There's lots of work to do around here. Dad will be home soon. Besides, there isn't much we don't know how to do. Mom let us do most things. I can make bread. I can cook. We'll keep up the garden and keep the stove going," Sara said taking charge of their situation.

"Maybe Daisy will have her kid soon. It would be nice to have milk again," said Mary as she watched the goats move around in their pen. "Do you think the cougar will come back and go after the goats?"

"Could. I'll load the gun and it will be ready, if we need it. Too bad Mom didn't take the gun. She may have had a chance if she had."

"You know how she hated guns. That's why Dad had you learn to shoot, Sara. You might have to shoot a deer for meat. Can you do it?"

Sara shook her head. "I don't know. We'd have to be pretty hungry before I could kill any more deer. We still have the chickens and they are laying a couple of eggs a day. And we can always fish. You're good at that."

Mary nodded slowly. She knew Sara was right. They would be okay until their father returned. She stifled her sobs and lifted her chin. "I know you can look after things. I can help. You're only two years older than I am, you know. Let's bring that old garden bench out to the point so we can go every day and check to see if Dad's coming."

"That's a good idea," agreed Sara. "Let's do that."

Together they maneuvered the gray weather-beaten bench to the point and set it up. The panoramic view of the bay and surrounding islands spread out before them.

"We could go for help," suggested Mary.

Sara snorted rudely. "How do you figure on doing that? It is at least five miles of rock, surf and cliffs between here and Thoresen's. We've only got the runabout. Besides, the old man is practically a hundred. What good would he be? We can't make it through the bush either. We'd get lost or the cougar will get us."

Mary burst into fresh tears. Sara rushed to her side and threw her arms around her. "I'm sorry, Mary. I'm sorry." She sat rocking her sister trying to comfort them both.

"No, the safest thing to do would be to wait for Dad. We will be careful with the flour and stuff. We can fish off our favorite rock and eat the chickens if we have to. We've got enough for a little while," Sara murmured.

They returned to the cabin. Sara stood looking out the kitchen window. The forest appeared to be nearer and the silence was deafening. She was only eighteen, but the weight of the world pressed down on her slender shoulders. She drew Mary into her arms and hugged her closer.

CHAPTER 21

KARL HAPPILY TOOLED AROUND THE BUSY HARBOR. THE CRAFT
felt sound and the engine needed only minor adjustments. Pumping
his fist in the air, he let out a holler. "Yah hoo!"

Turning quickly to the left, he headed further out into the ocean.
Just as he reached the headland, one engine coughed and died. Karl
bent over the controls struggling to restart the failed motor. To
his horror, the other engine began to stutter. Soon the boat was
bobbing listlessly in the rolling chuck.

No amount of fiddling with the fuel lines, starters or levers made
any difference. She was dead in the water. As the small boat drifted
further out past the headland, Karl knew he was in deep trouble.
There was no help for it. He called on the open channel for assistance from any boat in the vicinity. "Cabin cruiser disabled. Cabin
cruiser disabled. Position is just inside the harbor, leeward of Gallos
Point. Need a tow."

"Coast Guard cutter *Tynehead* responding. What's the name of
your vessel?"

"I haven't named it yet. Used to be *Gone Girl,* but it isn't registered anymore. I was taking it for a test run."

"Copy. Please give your name and describe the vessel."

"Karl Thoresen. Twenty-eight foot cabin cruiser. '79 Fiberform Executive. White hull with black trim."

"Roger. Are you without power?"

"Yes. Something's wrong with either the fuel line or the actual fuel. Engines checked out fine last night. The waves are tossing us around pretty good. The small kicker won't be able to make headway in this."

As he listened, Karl heard the Coast Guard hailing other boats that might be in the area. A fish boat was ten minutes away and another cabin cruiser was perhaps an hour out.

"*Tynehead* to Thoresen. *Tynehead* to Thoresen."

"Thoresen, here."

"Fish boat, the *Flying Eagle,* is on route to you now. Try to maintain position with the kicker. He should be visible in five to ten minutes. Let us know when you have a visual."

Twenty minutes later, Karl caught sight of the *Flying Eagle.* He radioed the Coast Guard that assistance was close at hand. As he waited anxiously for the fishing vessel, Karl wondered about the fuel line. Mentally he went over all the repairs. It seemed that he'd done everything right. The motors were fine yesterday. He'd scrubbed out the fuel tanks pretty good and there was little sign of rust in them. His suspicions deepened as he struggled to keep the boat facing the oncoming fish boat. *No, he'd done it all correctly. Must be the fuel itself. Either dirty diesel or someone had sabotaged his boat.*

"Ahoy, there. You Thoresen?" yelled the yellow slickered captain of the *Flying Eagle.*

"Yep, sure am. I'm mighty please to see you."

A few minutes later, the *Flying Eagle* had the crippled cruiser under tow. Karl and Dave, the captain of the *Flying Eagle,* were busy getting to know each other over a couple of bottles of beer. As they tied up to the marina, Karl offered to buy his rescuer some more brews at the bar across the street.

"Sure, why not. The old lady's in Prince and I've got the whole evening to kill."

Karl and his new best buddy headed over to a dingy watering hole identified only by a flashing neon sign and music blaring out of the door. Several beers later, neither man was feeling any pain. The incessant beat of country music grated on Karl's nerves.

"Can't stand anymore cowboy twang. Let's head over to the casino. I'm real good at Jack. Need to get some cash to cover the cost of the fuel line repairs. What do you say?"

"Nah, don't have much luck with cards," Dave whined. "Always lose my shirt."

"Sounds like you need some instruction, man. I can show you how to make a small fortune," Karl coaxed. "Come on. You can watch if you don't feel up to betting."

The two men wandered over to the casino. It was just shy of nine o'clock and the place was jumping. As Karl went through the doors, he meandered past the noisy slot machine section, scanning the crowd for his nemesis, George. No one looked remotely familiar.

Under Karl's instruction, Dave handily won five hundred and sixty dollars while Karl added well over six grand to his poke.

"Christ, you got horseshoes," exclaimed Dave as they counted their winnings in the parking lot. Neither of them heard quiet footsteps approaching. A bat connected with skull. Dave dropped like a brick.

"Want some of the action?"

Karl jerked around at the sound of a familiar voice. George stood off to one side as his henchman brandished a thick, wooden baseball bat.

"Been fleecing the house?" George snickered nodding to his back-up.

The bat swung catching Karl behind the knees bringing him down on all fours. Then pain radiated from the blow that struck across his shoulders. Vomiting onto the pavement, Karl reeled and bobbed trying to avoid being hit. Karl sagged, face forward on the pavement.

"Enough," commanded George. "Don't finish him off yet."

He reached down pulling Karl to his knees. With his face mere inches from Karl's, he growled. "Where've you been, buddy? Haven't seen you for well near five years. Been out of the country? Oh, yeah. Heard tell, you worked the joints in Lima for a while."

Karl was shocked. No one knew that he'd spent time in Lima. Quickly, he realized that George must be more connected than he had originally thought. "How the hell do you know where I've been?"

George guffawed. "The Kingdom Army has ties everywhere. You didn't think it's just in Canada did you? Nah, we are all over North and South America. Going to get into Thailand next."

"You mean I was working for Kingdom at that camp?" Karl winced as he tried to straighten his shoulders in an effort to look less frightened.

"Catch on fast, me boy. You ripped off more than Ren and the guys."

"I told you before. Ren and them took the money and dumped me in the bush. You gotta believe me," Karl pleaded with George. "I'd never take from the Kingdom. I didn't even know I was working for them."

"Now you do and now you owe…big time." George nodded again to his burly henchman. The blows hailed down.

Karl slumped into an unconscious heap.

Sirens wailed as police cars converged on the scene. The casino parking lot was always under surveillance.

"Call it in, Carmen. This one is definitely a scoop and run."

CHAPTER 22

KARL'S EYES OPENED. HE BECAME AWARE OF NIGGLING, PERSIS-
tent discomfort. A needle attached to clear tubing was boring itself
into the skin just above the inside of his right wrist. He shifted his
eyes scanning the rest of his arm. It seemed as though most of his
right arm was wrapped in soft beige elastic bandages. A loose sling
was wrapped around his shoulder.

Raising his left hand, he tried to brush off the intravenous. His
hand couldn't quite reach. He tried again, only to be held prisoner
by the metallic ring of a handcuff curving around the railings on
the bed.

He began to panic. He was unable to shift his head more than a
few inches in either direction. Some sort of apparatus was secured
to his head. *Where in hell was he and why couldn't he move?*

Warm agitation flooded his body. He could sense adrenaline
coursing his veins. He made attempts to move his legs. He could
move his feet slightly. Barely able to open his mouth, he managed a
faint whisper. Moans escaped his lips.

A nurse, summoned by beeps from the monitors wired to him,
hurried into the private ward. She crossed over the short space from
the doorway and examined the bank of machines. Small blips had

registered movement. Bending over Karl, she gently touched his hand. "Hey, you. Are you making it back to the land of the living?"

Karl's eyes fluttered open again. Again, he tried to talk.

"Take it easy," she said.

Her gentle voice drew him slowly out of his darkness.

"Your jaw is wired so you can't really talk much. Just nod your head if you can. Okay?"

"Thirsty," Karl managed to gasp.

The nurse held a straw to his mouth. "Just take small sips or you'll choke."

She activated the buzzer beside the bed. "Please let Dr. Aton know Mr. Thoresen has regained consciousness," she said as another nurse came over to the hospital bed. "Perhaps tell that cop outside the door, as well. He probably needs to let his superiors know."

After Dr. Anton had made a cursory examination, he raised the head of Karl's bed and allowed the detectives into the room.

"It is not my intention to protect this thug from your questions. As far as I'm concerned he is strong enough. In my country, this man would have been left to die. You Canadians waste time and money keeping scum like this alive." The doctor made it clear, to both Karl and to the police officers that he considered his job to be done.

Turning to the nurse, he barked his final orders.

"If he needs more pain medication refer him to the doctor on call. Get his transfer papers to rehab ready. We will move him as soon as possible."

Striding out of the room, Dr. Anton left Karl to face the police.

◇◇◇◇◇◇

A cat and mouse game began.

Suspecting that there was some kind of gang affiliation involved, Detective Rob proceeded with caution. He needed to get as much information out of Karl as possible, before his prisoner clammed up.

Karl sensed a trap. By now, he'd figured out where he was and was starting to remember the events that had put him here in hospital. Luckily, he could buy himself time. Time to think. Time to plan his next move.

Unable to speak more than single words at a time, he gave Detective Rob just enough information to throw him completely off the track.

The policeman left with the understanding that it had been a random attack by persons unknown to the victim. While it may have been gang related, Detective Rob was almost certain that Mr. Thoresen had no gang ties. He was just an unlucky sucker who had perhaps been mistaken for a rival gang member.

He removed the handcuff from Karl's wrist and rang for the nurse.

"We are going to release this man. No need to question him any further today. Give me a call at the station when he is ready to go home. We won't keep him cuffed. Besides he isn't going far in this condition. Two broken legs and a dislocated shoulder should keep him immobile for quite some time.

Later that evening, Penny, his night nurse came in. Gently she gave him a sponge bath and redressed his wounds.

He had a scalp full of stitches, legs broken in multiple places, a dislocated shoulder and severe bruising over most of his body.

"Sorry," she kept saying as Karl winced when she moved him. "You should feel a lot better this time next week."

"How long am I going to be cooped up here?" he asked, more than a little afraid of the answer.

"I imagine they'll move you to rehab soon. They need the beds. This is a ward for acute patients. You are out of danger so they'll probably move you tomorrow or the next day."

◇◇◇◇◇◇◇

After six interminable weeks in rehab, Karl was ready for outpatients. His only visitors had been George and Penny.

George came by once to see the damage for himself and a second time to remind Karl of his obligations. He made it clear that upon release, Karl would go back to work for him until the debt was paid off.

Karl recognized the debt would never be settled. He understood the ways of the Kingdom Army. Once you knew about them and their operations, there was no escaping their clutches. He began to firm up his plans.

Nurse Penny had taken a shine to him while he was at the hospital. She had dropped by to see him on a regular basis. Lately, their friendship had taken on a more romantic feel. Karl felt certain she could be persuaded to take him in for a brief time.

Her small apartment, part of an old rambling house on the outskirts of town, proved to be an excellent hiding place. Travelling after dark, they had arrived quietly and snuck in the back door. Her landlord hadn't seen him enter. While Penny was at work, Karl kept a very low profile. He did not venture out of the apartment. He left the television off and contented himself with reading books and sleeping.

Gradually he regained his strength. It was now time to fix the damn boat and get out of here.

Penny had discovered that Dave, the fish boat captain, had sustained only minor injuries. He had been treated and released the same night. She also learned that Dave was keeping the cabin cruiser tied up at his mooring until Karl contacted him.

"Hey man, remember me? It's Karl."

"How's it going? I would've come to see you except you keep really bad company," Dave said as soon as he realized who was calling. "I got your boat tucked in beside mine at the dock."

"Yes, I need to talk to you about that. See here, as you know I got problems with some guys here in town. The last thing I need is another round taken out of me. Think you could find me a spot away from prying eyes, where I can repair that cruiser?"

"Let me think on it. What's your number? I'll call you in a few days."

Much to Penny's disappointment, Karl moved out at the end of the week. It had been a nice walk in the sunshine, but now he had to get on with his plan. This plan included getting his hands on his uncle's money and fleeing the country. First, he'd get as far as L.A. and then he'd disappear into the Brazilian jungle.

◇◇◇◇◇◇

In the heat of the summer, sweating and cussing profusely, Karl stripped out the fuel lines; cleaned them and rescrubbed the tanks. He was right. The fuel had been contaminated with salt water. Once the water had hit the engines, they had seized. Trusting his instincts and remembering his uncle's lessons, Karl managed to fix the motors and fuel lines for less than four hundred bucks.

Karl sat on his deck of his boat thinking. His bank account was down to an uncomfortable three thousand. It would cost more than three grand to outfit this cruiser and purchase enough supplies for a long trip. Navigation equipment was subpar on the '79. New gear would cost a fortune, but he wasn't about to rely on used safety equipment when he motored down this rough coastline. Dave needed someone to replace his lead hand since the man had jumped ship to work for a rival boat. Maybe this was his answer. He'd ask about hiring on for a bit, in the morning.

His main goal was to get to Thoresen Island, but there were no guarantees that once there, he'd find what he was looking for. Maybe the old bugger was broke. He highly doubted it. Both his old man and his uncle had been pretty cagey with money. Sven probably had a bucket load stuffed somewhere.

◇◇◇◇◇◇

Seven months later, Karl was ready. "I'll take it all in cash. Close out the account," he told the teller.

"That's a lot of money to carry around, sir. Are you sure you don't want a bank draft or for us to transfer it to your next account?"

"No, I'll take cash and no bigger than hundreds, please."

Karl took the large envelope of cash and stuffed it into his duffel bag. Striding out of the bank, he made for the dock and the safety of his newly outfitted boat.

Dave was waiting for him.

"Well, I'm off," Karl said as he shook Dave's hand. He pressed several c-notes into the man's outstretched palm. "I thank you, sir.

You've kept up your end of the bargain. You've got Tom to fish with you now and I've got to make tracks."

"Take care. Don't run into any more baseball bats." Dave untied the lines and Karl fired up the motors.

◇◇◇◇◇◇◇

Karl inched his way down the coast staying close to shore, ducking in and out of bays and inlets. Knowing that he couldn't trust anyone, he kept out of sight of most marine traffic. There was no real hurry and he was safe so long as the Kingdom didn't clue in to his escape plan.

They had bigger concerns. A nasty turf war had started up, just before he'd left. He'd heard that the Kingdom was struggling to maintain its hold on the northern casinos. Their rivals had more manpower and more connections.

He chuckled and fervently hoped that George was up to his pasty little neck in the whole mess.

CHAPTER 23

STRAINING HER EYES TO SEE THROUGH THE SHEETING RAIN, SHE caught a glimpse of a shadowy shape. Blood dripped and pooled on the path in front of her. The shape moved again, this time weaving back and forth as if beckoning to her. Blood spattered now; shaken from open jaws. Small baby limbs reached out in supplication. As the stench of cat urine threatened to overwhelm her, Mary screamed. "Sara! Sara!"

⬦⬦⬦⬦⬦⬦

Wearily Sara rolled over on the bed and held Mary tightly. The nightmare subsided. This was the third time Mary had woken up screaming. Neither of them had slept soundly in the two days following the cougar's attack.

In the morning, Sara could tell there was something different about Mary. Her eyes were a dull slate colour with no hint of recognition. "Mary. Mary," she said softly. "Everything is okay now. You just had lots of bad dreams last night."

No response. "Mary, come and eat. I've made your favorite, scrambled eggs. Come and eat."

No response. Mary sat rocking slightly, staring into space. Her bare feet stuck out from beneath her nightdress. Her fingers curled around a greasy lock of blonde hair.

"Mary, snap out of it!" Sara said sternly. "Come on, this is enough. You have to help yourself. I can't be strong for both of us all the time."

No response. Sara began to weep softly to herself. She was on her last nerve. No one had ever prepared her for something like this. First her mother and baby brother had been killed and now Mary seemed to have disappeared leaving this vacant, staring zombie in her place.

"Dad, Dad where are you?" she whimpered into her hands. "What am I supposed to do now?" She raised her head and stared at Mary. Kindness, stern voice or coaxing— nothing was making any difference this time. She decided to put Mary into their parents' bed and leave her be.

During the long sleepless night, she had resolved that the shed was not an ideal place to leave the bodies. If the cougar was still around, it might be attracted to the odours. She was going to have to move Anna and Samuel.

After taking an old tarp from under the pile of building materials, she removed Mary's sign and opened the shed door. Cool air met her face as she peered into the dimly lit shack. Dragging the tarp behind her, she crossed over to the faded blue that held the remains of her mother and her baby brother. Steeling herself, she rolled the bodies onto the tarp and pulled the shroud around them. Heaving the unwieldy burden with her, she left the shed. It took all her strength, but eventually she managed to load it into her dad's makeshift wheelbarrow. The wobbly front wheel nearly buckled under the weight.

With the wheelbarrow threatening to run away on her, she eased it slowly down the steep trail to the beach and over towards the point. She had to stop several times to catch her breath as she strained to control the barrow. The sun was pounding down on her unprotected head.

She arrived at a small outcropping of rocks. She wedged the bundle in as far it would go, inside a shallow cave. It took a couple of hours to shore up the entrance with boulders and driftwood. Exhausted, she returned to the cabin to check on Mary.

Mary was sitting in Anna's rocking chair with her doll cradled in her arms. She was dressed in one of Anna's housedresses, humming softly to the doll. She lifted her head and smiled at her sister. "Hi, where were you?"

Sara crossed over to her sister and took her into her arms. Realizing that Mary had no recollection of the past few hours, she spoke carefully. "I took Mom and Samuel to a new place where they'll be safer. You know that hollow under the rocks by the beach. Do you want to come and put your sign there?"

Mary's eyes reflected confusion and then remembrance. "Okay."

She got up and put on her rubber boots. "Let's go."

The sisters placed the sign on top of the outcropping of rocks. Mary held Sara's hand as they recited the only real prayer they knew: The Lord's Prayer.

◇◇◇◇◇◇

Mary shrieked, "A boat! Sara, a boat!"

Sara rushed from the garden to their bench. Sure enough there was a small blip on the horizon. They watched as the vessel came closer, turn and venture towards their homestead. As it grew closer, it was obviously not the fish boat. It was not Dad coming home. Disappointment washed over her.

"It's too small. It must be the Coast Guard," Sara murmured as she took in the shape and size of the oncoming boat.

Unable to cope, Mary threw a despairing look at Sara and rushed off up the path towards their cave, her sanctuary.

"Hi," Jennifer said cheerfully as she jumped onto the dock. "Where is everyone?"

At the sound of Jennifer's lilting voice, Sara collapsed sobbing into the young woman's arms. Through gasping sobs, Sara managed to tell Jennifer and Steven what had happened since their last visit.

When Sara finished her horrible story, Steven went to find the cave and to bring Mary back. Jennifer built up the fire in the wood stove and set the kettle to boil. Sara washed her face and slowly composed herself. She needed to be strong. She didn't want Mary to see her in such a state.

"Well, I found your cave, but I can't get her to come down with me," Steven said as he came through the cabin door. "She just moved back further into the cave and hugged the wall. She won't budge."

"I'll go see to her. Sometimes, you just have to let her be until she's ready to face people. That was one of the reasons why we moved here. Mary was bullied unmercifully because of her face...she was beaten and tormented, most of her high school year. Moving here has been wonderful for her, until now." With that explanation, Sara left for the cave.

"Mary, it's me. Come out to where I can see you properly."

Mary shuffled over to Sara. "I don't want anyone to see my cow face," she whimpered. "Make them go away, please," she begged.

"Come on. You know Steven and Jennifer, the Coast Guard people. They've seen your face before and they're not bothered. Besides, it's going to get dark soon. You know it's too dangerous to be here by yourself in the dark."

"I don't want to see anyone. No. Please don't make me."

"Mary, come on. Let's get down to the cabin. Jennifer's making tea," Sara pleaded.

Eventually, Mary agreed to return to the cabin, but as soon as she got there, she went straight through to the girls' room and crawled into bed fully clothed.

Sara and her friends talked quietly most of the night. Sara filled them in with all the details of the cougar attack, the bullying and Mary's problem.

"Well, we just can't leave you here alone to wait for your father," Steven told Sara. "You are two young girls and this is far too isolated. You can't manage even for a little while."

Sara bristled at his words. "Most people my age wouldn't be okay, but I'm not most people. I helped build this homestead. I know how to fix just about everything. The garden is mine. I chopped most of that wood you see beside the door. I can do whatever is needed for the two of us."

"What if the cougar comes back?"

"Dad taught me how to shoot. I'm not keen on hunting deer, but I can fish and so can Mary. The goats are penned at night and so are the chickens. I can shoot the cougar if it comes again. Likely, it's travelled on. We haven't seen any tracks. I've been looking."

Steven had to agree on that point. The cougar had probably moved on or it would have been back by now. Cougars were mostly absent from this part of the coast.

"There's Mary to think about. You have both been through a lot. You need support and you should be around other people," Jennifer added quietly. "Mary needs professional help."

"Those so called professionals didn't help her much before. All the tranquilizers, psychotherapy and specialists made no difference at all. That's mainly the reason we decided to come here," Sara stated flatly. "This was working. Living here was getting her better."

The group fell silent for a while. Wood crackled in the stove and Mary's soft snoring drifted from the other room. Everyone sat lost in their own thoughts. Sara rested her head on her arms. The warm cabin and the desperate late night conversation were exhausting her. "You guys, go rest in Mom and Dad's room. I'll go in with Mary."

◇◇◇◇◇◇

Steven and Jennifer talked in hushed whispers as they lay beside each other on top of the small double bed.

"Sam will be back by the end of October at the latest. I can't imagine his coming home to an empty cabin and finding out about his wife and baby from a letter. Then not having the rest of his family for comfort. Besides, what will happen to the goats and chickens? Sara's right. It would be best if they wait for him," Jennifer said reluctantly.

"Sara's strong, but maybe not strong enough. Mary could get worse."

"She could," agreed Jennifer, "but I doubt that moving back to the mainland will help right now. She probably needs to process this crisis. She might really go off the deep end if she goes back too soon."

Steven sighed. "I don't like it. Remember, we are reassigned for the winter months— starting next month."

"We'll leave the details with head office. Besides, Sam will be back by then."

◇◇◇◇◇◇

With Steven and Jennifer following her around the homestead, Sara explained all their winter preparations, how the water and power system worked, and their emergency plans.

"The satellite phone is not great, but it does work sometimes."

"Here, let me check it out," Steven held out his hand. "There looks as though there might be some corrosion around the battery terminal." He spent the better part of an hour going over the equipment. "You did renew the contract, didn't you?"

Sara assured him it was part of the safety plan their father had put in place before they even left the city. "It's an automatic renewal… the money comes out of the bank account each year. We also have the basic supplies like flour, sugar and stuff delivered twice a year by which ever boat is heading this way. Usually, the supplies come in with the Koreans when they pick up Dad for the fishing season. Our family has pretty much thought of everything."

"Well, here you go. I can't see much wrong with it except the corrosion. Maybe the battery doesn't hold much of a charge anymore." Steven passed the cumbersome phone over to Sara. "You should charge it up from the generator more frequently and get your dad to get a back-up battery. I'm going to see if I can trace the Korean boat through the Coast Guard channels. Do you know its name or call letters?"

"No. The only markings on the boat were two eyes painted on the bow. There were numbers and letters, but I never paid much attention."

"Well, some of these vessels are pretty sketchy with their registrations. I'll do my best. They might well be out of range." Steven smiled ruefully. "Hopefully, your dad calls to check up on you guys. He's due back by the end of the month anyway."

◇◇◇◇◇◇◇

Mary was fine in the morning. It was as if her panicked flight to the cave had never happened. She chatted with Jennifer and shyly served Steven a third cup of coffee.

Steven glanced at Jennifer and smiled. He was relieved to see this change in Mary. It was making their leaving so much easier.

Mary stood chatting to Sara as they watched Jennifer and Steven leap aboard the Coast Guard vessel. They waved until they could no longer see the young guards' faces as the cutter chugged its way out past the headland. Turning as one, the sisters went back up to the cabin. As always, there was work to be done. The cool autumn winds tousled their hair and raised the hope that Dad would be returning soon.

Chapter 24

THE SEAS MOVED AS SLICK AS A ROLLER COASTER AT THE FAIR. ONE minute the vessel idled in the churning sea and the next it was thrust skyward only to career down the wave into the next trough. Sheets of water drenched the deck. The coursing water was threatening to sweep the crew off their feet. Only their safety lines latched to the railings gave any support. As each wave hit, the vessel shuddered and corrected itself.

Unable to understand the frantic commands shouted in Korean, Sam could do little to help. He was a mechanic not a sailor. Keeping out of the way of the desperate battle raging around him, he hung on for dear life.

Grim faces of the Koreans betrayed their fear. Loud voices mixed with the howling winds as orders were shouted. Each seaman bent to his task, intent on riding out the storm.

◇◇◇◇◇◇

Towards dawn the storm abated leaving the fish boat slogging through the swells. As the morning came full upon them, Sun Soon-Chun faced his crew. These men relied on him. Their families depended on him and his ability to return their menfolk safely. In Korean, he thanked them for overcoming the storm and then promised to head to the nearest port. They would spend the winter months in Seattle. They could sell what fish they had to the American markets and return to their loved ones in the spring.

A clamor of dissension rose as the men understood that they would now be away from home for the next six months. Unwilling to risk the lives of his crew and the safety of his vessel, Sun Soon-Chun held firm. Each man was allowed two minutes on the radio to transmit a message home.

◇◇◇◇◇◇

Sam held the radio in his hand and pressed the call button. He left a message with the port authorities to be relayed to his family via the next boat heading past the homestead. This was his only hope of getting a message through to them, since he knew the family didn't monitor the radio frequencies and only used the satellite in emergencies. His heart sank as he realized he would not see Anna and the children until spring.

Unexpectedly, just outside of Hammond Inlet, a rogue wave hit. The crew scrambled to reattach safety lines as the water suddenly smashed against the hull sending the crew sliding portside. Tilting dangerously, the vessel managed to right itself flinging Sun Soon-Chun and another seaman into the swirling chuck.

Fighting his way through the sailors gripping the railing, Sam watched as first the seaman disappeared and then Sun Soon-Chun fell beneath the sea. Desperately, he wrestled free the ropes that lashed the tender to the side of the fish boat. He jumped in and gestured to the crew to lower the tiny runabout.

Straining his eyes, he scanned the black surface looking for the men. Kelp, foam and the dull swirling waves made it impossible to see any sign of the captain or the crew member. As he turned back towards the fish boat, another wave slammed the vessel sending it careening towards the tender. With a sickening crunch, the small craft was sucked under the hull. It reappeared moments later.

Sam was gone.

◇◇◇◇◇◇◇

Shin Jong-kyi, the first mate, steered the boat into Seattle. He reported the captain's death and that of the crewman, but did not say anything about Sam. Sam had been working without papers and Shin Jong-kyi feared authority. He, himself was an illegal, working without immigration status. He wanted no trouble.

CHAPTER 25

KARL MOTORED ALONG SLOWLY ENJOYING THE FALL WEATHER, THE peace, quiet and freedom that had been absent over the past few months. No one knew his whereabouts and better yet no one cared. His only concerns were catching fish for his evening meal and drinking enough whiskey to get a buzz on. Days passed in a soft blur. Nights were filled with dreams of Beth, his lady in the woods, and more recently Penny, his latest lover. While he did miss female company, he knew it was only a matter of time before he got his hands on the Thoresen money. He could then head for a tropical paradise. There would be plenty of women to spend his money on and lots of games to conquer. Thoresen money would be his stake in the future. Right now, he relished the warmth of the sun on his face and the isolation of this rugged coastline.

A slight movement on a narrow point of land jutting out to sea caught his attention. As the cabin cruiser drew nearer, Karl cut the engine and drifted. Bobbing in the gentle swells, he watched as a black wolf sniffed amongst the smooth pebbles lining the beach. Its fur glistened in the afternoon sun.

Sensing his presence, the wolf lifted its head.

A feral stare met Karl's eyes.

Karl's heart leapt. Freedom, wilderness and pride were communicated in an eternal moment.

Slowly, the animal assessed the intruder. Discerning no threat, the wolf returned to his search. Jaws crunched an unlucky crab; splintering the silent scene. With a glance at his visitor, the wolf turned and trotted noiselessly into the surrounding scrub.

Karl laughed as he realized he had been holding still for the last ten minutes, unwilling to break the magic.

That night, as he tossed fitfully in his narrow bunk, Karl thought about his childhood home, his adventures with Uncle Sven, and yearned for the simple past that had long been denied. Visions of feral eyes and glistening fur punctuated his reverie. Harsh realities rose to meet these fond memories.

Uncle Sven had broken up his family. His mother had turned her back on her husband and her child in favour of her lover. That had been the end of his idyllic childhood. As his father grew more and more morose, he remembered being more of a burden than a son. He recalled many days, towards the end of his time at the homestead, when no words were spoken between father and son. It was little wonder he left as soon as he could.

He hadn't seen his uncle in years. He doubted if Sven even knew of his brother's passing. Rumours had it that the old man was virtually a hermit now. Maybe he wasn't on Thoresen Island any more. Karl shook his head. No, the old bugger must still be there. Where would he go? He had to be there…that money was rightfully his. Sure, he'd got the money from his father's estate, but the lawyers wouldn't know about any hidden assets. He was going to get the rest of his inheritance one way or another.

◇◇◇◇◇◇

Watching clouds gathering on the horizon, he knew that the winter storms were closing in. This coast was plagued by violent winter weather. Most travel ceased at this time of the year with ships sheltering in various ports to wait for spring. Even the Coast Guard service was reduced to emergency runs. Their usual patrols were curtailed by late October or early November.

Topping up his fuel tanks from barrels lining his deck, Karl raised the anchor and set off in the direction of Thoresen Island. He could easily reach the area in less than a week.

Meanwhile, he schemed and plotted the tale he would tell Sven. It had to be believable. He would tap into the wonderful times they had spent before the split. He could tell Sven that his father had forbidden him to contact him and now that his father had passed on, he was trying to make amends. *Yes, that might work. The old guy was probably as lonely as hell. Uncle Sven might welcome him with open arms. Open arms and open pocket book.*

Chapter 26

WEEKS PASSED AS THE GIRLS COMPLETED THEIR PREPARATIONS for winter. Working tirelessly in the garden, they managed to harvest the remainder of the crops. Carrots, potatoes and corn were piled into cribs in the cave. All the foodstuffs that were delivered by Sun Soon-Chun in the fall, were now stored in there as well.

"Dad will be pleased that we've done such a good job," Sara said to Mary as they sat on their cliff side bench sipping tea.

"Yes, he would," agreed Mary. "I'm getting worried, though. I thought he'd be back by now."

"Me, too. It's near the end of October and the seas are getting rougher. The geese stopped flying over two weeks ago."

Mary lowered her head. "You know, it's is all my fault. We wouldn't be in this mess...Mom wouldn't be dead and Dad would be here...if it wasn't for me. I'm just such a coward. I should have stood up to Sharon...I should have..."

"Hush. Don't go on like this. We were all happy here. What happened to Mom and Samuel wasn't your fault. It just happened." She gathered her sister into her arms. "We'll get through this. We have to."

◇◇◇◇◇◇

In the small meadow beside the creek, Sara and Mary began to swing the scythes, cutting the wild grasses. Resting every now and then, they managed to cut the half-acre patch.

"I can't imagine doing a much bigger field with these scythes. Can you? Friggin hard work," complained Sara.

Mary shrugged.

Sara had noticed that Mary seldom complained lately and seemed to be taking on far more than her share of the chores. It was as if she was trying to make amends. As though, she was trying to make Sara's life easier.

Suddenly, Mary clapped her hands and threw down the rake she was using. "I have an idea. Let's bring a tarp up and load the grass onto it. If we bundle it up, we could get the whole lot down in one go. We can't just push it over the hill or we will lose half to the wind."

Sara grinned. Mary had a good idea.

They shrieked with laughter as they hurled the blue bundle off the top of the hill. It landed smack in the middle of the squash patch. The plants were ruined, but it didn't really matter. It was time to bring the squash in anyway. Frost had already touched the flower garden and was threatening the sheltered garden patch. Soon the wild grasses were piled beside the goat shed. They would use these grasses to supplement the precious grains they had to feed to the goats over the winter.

"Here, Daisy, here," encouraged Sara as she held out a handful of grass. "Got to make milk for Sassy." As the little goat butted at her mother's udder Sara called to her. "Okay, Sassy girl, leave mama alone for now. You can have some too."

Finishing up the supper dishes, Sara glanced out the cabin door. She was constantly on the alert. Where was Mary now? She stepped out onto the porch and looked around. Even though it was past dusk and there was no possibility of seeing a boat in the darkness, Mary was still sitting on their bench with her knees up and arms wrapped tightly around her legs. She crossed over to the seat. "Mary, no one is coming tonight. Come on in and we'll play some Scrabble."

◇◇◇◇◇◇

By the end of November, the girls' hopes of their father coming home for the winter were fading. "Do you think he is okay?" stammered Mary. She had been sobbing since she had gotten up that morning. "Perhaps we should call Jennifer and Steven to see if they have heard anything."

"I'll charge the satellite phone. We still have quite a bit of fuel left for the generator." They had been conserving fuel since the last delivery in the fall. After a long while the green light appeared on the device. The girls drew on their heavy, red and black checkered lumberman shirts and rubber boots. Sara grabbed the piece of paper with the Coast Guard number.

Sitting on 'satellite rock', the huge boulder on top of the cliff where they could usually get a good signal, the girls put in a call to the Coast Guard station. They were dismayed to hear that Jennifer and Steven had already gone to their winter assignment.

Rob Fielding, the operator, was new to the area and had no real idea who the Lindholm girls were. He searched through a stack of papers on his desk. He remembered seeing a message from a Sam Lindholm.

The phone began cutting out. As Rob Fielding began to relay the message from their father, the equipment failed completely.

Horrified, the sisters gaped at the machine. Mary grabbed the phone and shook it violently.

"Here let me see," shouted Sara reaching for the phone. Her hand lunged forward.

The phone slipped from Mary's grasp and fell in a sweeping arc down over the cliff, bouncing off the rocks and crashing into the sea. Suspended in the moment, they watched as their only link to civilization sank beneath the waves.

"Oh, my God," whispered Mary. "What was the message? What did Dad say?"

"We have to know what the message was. We just have to."

Later that night as they sat around the stove, the sisters decided that they should go to Thoresen Island and ask the old man if he could contact the Coast Guard for the message.

"The seas are getting way too rough," exclaimed Sara trying to be sensible. "We will get the runabout ready and then wait for a calm day."

They waited for well over a week and the only difference in the seas was that they were getting more turbulent. Unable to wait any longer, the sisters put on their life jackets and set off towards Thoresen Island. Their small bay posed no problems, but as they rounded the headland the off-shore winds hit them with full force. The small runabout heaved and pitched as the waves threatened to capsize the tiny craft.

Quickly, Sara reached over and hooked the tether strap of her life jacket to Mary's. "Hang on, Mary, hang on."

Heading into the waves, Sara frantically tried to calculate her best course of action. It was impossible to turn around without being hit broadside by the oncoming waves. It was too dangerous to keep heading out into the strait between their homestead and the island.

In an instant, the decision was taken out of her hands. As the next wave crashed over their bow, both girls were thrown out into the churning sea.

Shock turned to panic as their bodies were dragged further and further into the frigid water. Sara, blinded by the stinging salt water, reached out instinctively towards her younger sister. Forcing her eyes open, she caught sight of Mary inches away.

Her mouth was open as if she were in the midst of singing, her eyes stark with terror. Mary grabbed Sara and flailing with her sneaker burdened feet, she fought to bring them both to the surface.

Horror struck, they watched the runabout disappear beneath the waves. Not a trace was left.

Gasping and choking, they clung to each other as the waves battered them. Cold and shock were starting to take their toll. Icy waves stole their breath. Survival instincts kicked in. The sisters turned as a unit and desperately started swimming towards the nearest land.

"Come on, Sara, keep going. We're nearly there. We're nearly there." Struggling against the pull of the undertow snaking past the headland, they finally reached the outcropping of rocks that formed the point of their bay. Numb fingers scrabbled to find purchase on cruel, jagged, barnacle-encrusted rocks. They dragged their freezing bodies up and out of the sea.

Wheezing and spluttering as they lay on the shallow ledge, the girls were growing colder by the second. "Get up, get up, Sara. We can't lie here, we'll die. You've got to get up, now."

They clung to each other as they staggered across the rocks towards the distant sandy beach in front of the homestead. Mary scarcely glanced at the burial site as she half dragged and half carried her sister.

Sara and Mary were spent by the time they reached the steep path to the cabin. The effort of crossing the rocks had warmed their feet slightly, but had left them exhausted. Only the beckoning promise of shelter kept them going.

"Strip, strip," Mary pleaded as they fell through the doorway. "We have to get out of these wet clothes. The fire is out. We have to get warm somehow."

"Emergency kit," stuttered Sara. "Space blankets...those silver things in the packets."

Huddling under Anna's quilt, wrapped in the crinkly space-aged material, the sisters finally began warming up.

Sara reached her arm around Mary. "Thank you, thank you. You were the strong one, this time. You saved my life. Oh God, Mary, you saved my life." Sobbing softly, she hugged Mary close, drifting off to sleep as the goats bleated forlornly inside their shed.

Dusk had settled by the time Sara woke. Reluctantly, she shrugged out of the warm cocoon that surrounded them. Putting on her favorite sweat pants and top, she set about lighting the fire. Soon she was feeding larger kindling into its maw. Sighing with satisfaction, she stood basking in the heat that radiated from the reliable old stove.

"Up you get, Mary. I warmed up some soup. We need to get some food inside us."

As they sat spooning their soup, the goats began their pathetic bleating again. "Give over, Daisy. Give over. I'll be there in a while." Sara closed her eyes savouring the delicious broth. Time stood still as the girls enjoyed the simple meal. They were grateful to be alive, to be warm and to have each other.

The next morning, the stark truth of their situation sank in as the girls sat around the rough-hewn table taking stock. Rapidly, they came to the realization that without a boat and satellite phone, they were stuck at the homestead for the winter. They made plans.

Sara was determined to put a positive spin on their plight. "Mom and Dad have taught us well. We can easily make it even if Dad doesn't come until spring. There's plenty of food and no one will get sick. Heck, we've survived nearly drowning. We can survive anything."

She shuddered at the memory of how close they had come to dying. Her sleep that night had been punctuated by flashbacks of Mary's open mouth and the dark sea closing in over their heads.

"I've got my painting and you can work on your spinning and your high school courses. We'll be fine until Dad comes and then we'll decide what to do. Now that Mom's gone, he may want to go back to the city. After all, his dream is shattered. He may want to go back."

"Sara, I'm never going back to the city. I will stay here with Dad when he comes back. I'll even stay here by myself if the two of you decide to leave."

"Don't be silly. No one can stay on by themselves."

"I can. Going back is something I won't do. I'll kill myself first."

Sara sat and listened as Mary, totally lucid, gave her a rare glimpse into her tortured world. She told in vivid detail the horror of the beatings and words that had scorched her soul. She described wounds that reached into her very core; that had convinced her that she was worthless...totally worthless.

"Here I have peace. Here I can feel the sunshine warming my skin. I can touch the waves. I can live in the stillness. Here we are a family. We have each other. I don't need anyone else."

Sara sighed inwardly. She could see unmasked fear in her sister's eyes. However, she was unable to deny her mixed feelings and pondered the future. Part of her yearned for the outside world filled with people other than her family. She wondered what it would be like to know a man. She yearned to have a loving relationship similar to the one her parents had. She was proud of her paintings. If she stayed, who would ever see them?

Then remembering her promise to her father, she knew she must always take care of her little sister. Dad would decide what to do. Until then, she needed to keep Mary safe. "We'll be fine. The Koreans are probably riding out the winter somewhere near Seattle or San Francisco. Dad will be back in the spring and Jennifer and Steven too. All we have left to do before winter is to insulate the goat shed and to shore up those boards around the chicken house. Let's get at that tomorrow."

Mary grabbed her coat and went out to feed the animals.

Sara watching her go, smiled ruefully to herself. If Mary stayed in her present state of mind the winter would be tolerable. She knew the chances of that happening were very slim. Her sister often showed signs of getting better only to crash days later. Long periods of silence and constant rocking with occasional uncontrolled sobbing were very hard to endure. Still, it was Mary who had saved them when the boat sank. She would be forever grateful to her sister for showing strength when it was really needed. Perhaps it was a sign that Mary was gaining some measure of control. Once again, she cursed Sharon and all the havoc those nasty girls had wrought.

CHAPTER 27

TOWARDS THORESEN ISLAND THE LANDFORMS BEGAN TO LOOK slightly familiar. It had been years since he'd set eyes on this part of the coast. The compass and GPS indicated that given his present rate of speed, he'd be there in less than two days. He rechecked his positioning and tossed the anchor for the night. The seas were becoming rougher and winter was settling over this jagged land. He would be glad to make landfall.

Throttling back the engines, he slowly rounded the small bay and began coasting towards a dilapidated dock. No one seemed to be around. "Hello, hello. Uncle Sven, hello." Silence. Karl called again.

"I heard you the first time, you son of a bitch. Who the hell are you?"

Karl stared first at the barrel of a shotgun and then at the decrepit old codger who held him in its sights. "Hey, Uncle Sven. Don't you recognise me? It's Karl, your nephew Karl."

"Karl? Harry's boy?"

"Yep. Karl."

The old man strained to see Karl's face more clearly. It was obvious that his sight was failing. The gun was more of a prop that anything else. "Well, I'll be. What you here for? Thought you'd dropped off the face of the earth after your mom died. What you here for?"

"Let me come ashore and I'll fill you in on everything. Am I ever glad to see you."

Karl tied up his boat and cautiously approached the old man. The shotgun was still pointed at his chest. "No need for protection," Karl said waving at the gun. "You remember me Uncle Sven. *I come in peace*," Karl joked using the old Star Wars quote that had been a favorite of theirs when everyone still lived together at the homestead. "*I come in peace.*"

A smile wreathed the wrinkled face and the gun was lowered. Tears trickled down his weathered cheeks as Sven reached out to hug his long lost nephew.

Karl refilled both glasses. Sitting here, in front of a wood stove jawing with his uncle, melted time away. He had been fond of his father's brother. They'd spent many days together rambling through the forest which had bordered the homestead. It was from Sven, he'd learned most of his survival skills and a lot of those mechanical skills that had stood him in good stead.

Sven had been the one to counsel him when he was going through his turbulent teen years. His uncle had enjoyed the luxury of being the 'good guy' in the eternal war of parenting. It seemed to Karl that his father had almost relished the 'bad guy' role. No wonder his mother had preferred Sven. Still, Karl found it impossible to truly forgive her for abandoning him. Again, he put the most of blame on his father. If the marriage had been happier, she might not have strayed.

As the evening wore on, the men softened their stance. Each ruminated on old memories and each dwelt in the past. The fire died to faint coals as the booze took effect. Finally, nearly comatose with fatigue and liquor, both men called it a night. Karl's last thought as he drifted off to sleep, in the narrow cot beside the stove, was that this was going to be easier than he'd imagined.

As the sun came up Karl found himself nursing a sickening hangover. He climbed gingerly out of bed and made his way to the outhouse. This was his first chance to look around Sven's property.

Many of the old buildings were in various stages of disrepair. The animal sheds still held onto the faint odours of their long ago occupants. A shallow garden plot looked as though it needed a good tilling. However, the cabin itself appeared to be in half decent shape and the outhouse stood solid against the elements.

Supper last night had been some kind of fish stew with potatoes as a starch. Karl suspected the old guy subsisted on whatever he could grow or catch. By the look of him, he wasn't faring too badly. The old codger didn't have an ounce of fat on his body, but he didn't have any sores from malnutrition either.

Karl jumped aboard his cruiser and entered the galley. Soon, he returned to the cabin carrying a steaming pot in his hand. "Hey, Uncle Sven, I made porridge. Let's dull that booze headache." He ladled heaping portions into chipped bowls and set them on the table.

◇◇◇◇◇◇

Sven glanced at his nephew. It had been a long time since he'd seen any family. He'd sorely missed the young man after the break up. Didn't miss his son of a bitch brother but he had missed Karl. "How's your dad doing?" he asked reluctantly. "How's Harry?"

"Dad died in hospital seven years ago. Died of cancer."

"Oh. So what've you been doing in the meantime?"

Karl launched into a sanitized version of the intervening years. He didn't mention the gambling or the troubles he'd had with the mob. He spun tales of ladies, travelling and adventures.

Sven listened, enthralled by Karl's exciting life. He especially enjoyed the travel stories as his one regret was not having travelled abroad himself.

"Stone cold broke, though," complained Karl as he wound up his stories. "Travel and ladies aren't cheap."

Sven cleared his throat. Ever suspicious and guarded in money matters, he casually glanced towards Karl. Keeping a poker face, he said his piece. "No money left here, I'm afraid. Harry and I split the poke and I spent most of mine looking after your mother. Nothing could fix her. What a miserable way to die." The old man lapsed into daydreams of what might have been.

◇◇◇◇◇◇◇

Karl shook his head incredulously. From what he understood, Sven could not have spent his money finding a cure for his mother. She'd died too quickly. It had been a fast moving disease, whatever it was. *Cagey old bastard was as tight fisted as most of the rest of his Swedish family.*

"Going to do some fishing," he said getting up and going out the door. Climbing aboard his cruiser, he set off to the entrance of the bay. Dropping his lines, he trolled for the rest of the afternoon coming back with three nice salmon.

"My eyes don't see too well to filet anymore. Have to do it mostly by feel these days. You got any flour on your boat? I could rustle up some bannock and we could have a fry up," Sven offered, as Karl began to gut and filet the first salmon.

Later that evening, Karl brought up most of his supplies from the boat. Sven had said he could stop until spring if he wanted. This suited Karl fine. He had nowhere better to go. Besides, the money had to be here somewhere. No place else for it to be.

Carefully making sure the old man drank more whisky than he did, Karl had lots of opportunities to search the cabin and outbuildings whenever Sven was sleeping it off.

He methodically scoured every conceivable hiding place in the cabin, moving on to the animal sheds and eventually the outhouse. Frustrated with his unsuccessful results, he began to badger Sven who had never trusted the banks. "Where'd you stash it?" He joked as he scrutinized the old guy's face for any hint of the cache's location.

Sven never blinked. He never wavered in his insistence that it was all gone.

Unable to shake the feeling that his uncle was hiding the truth, Karl grew more and more aggravated. Several times he nearly gave himself away as he pumped the old guy for information. Thankfully,

Karl realized his uncle's rapidly failing eyesight missed most of his unconscious grimaces, clenched fists and tightened jawline. Spring was coming. Karl needed money.

Growing increasingly frustrated, he peppered Sven about the brothers' luck in the gold fields. "What happened to your share? Dad had lots left when he croaked. Christ, he gave the cancer society several grand and there was still some left over." He lied, inventing more and more ways that his father had been well off.

Sven snorted. "How come you didn't get any of it? You're the one bellyaching about being broke."

"He didn't know where I was for a while. Then by the time he was in hospital, it was too late to change his will. I inherited the homestead. Useless piece of land. Got very little when I sold it to a hippy, dippy family seven years ago. Money barely took me to Peru."

Karl kept badgering his uncle. "You took at least half of the money when you left with Mom. Where did it all go? Don't tell me you spent it on her. She didn't last that long. What did you do with it? It doesn't take much to live here on the island. Don't tell me it's all gone."

Karl stepped around the kitchen table and grabbed Sven's filthy undershirt. Dragging the man towards him, he sputtered angrily. "I need money. You gotta loan me some money."

Sven's eyes widened and with surprising strength, he pushed Karl's hand away. "That ain't no way to get a loan, my boy. I told you I haven't got any money left. You can't have what I don't have. There is no money here. Leave me alone or take yourself off this island. I don't like it when you're like this. You can leave for all I care. Good riddance."

Knowing he'd over stepped his mark, Karl immediately sought to restore peace. Burying his head in his hands, he muttered. "Christ, I'm sorry. Don't know what came over me, Uncle Sven. Sorry. It's just that I need money so God damn bad." He poured each of them a shot, downing his in one gulp.

◇◇◇◇◇◇

Sven's condition weakened rapidly over the next few weeks. From a reasonably robust man, he morphed into a bed-ridden invalid who rattled and moaned throughout the night. The small cabin reeked of sweat and urine. Karl could see what was happening. Sven was dying just like his father had done in hospital. It was only a matter of time.

He spoon-fed his uncle and did whatever personal care that was needed. The long days and nights became one as Karl waited for the end. As Sven lapsed into that dreamy state between conscious and not, Karl renewed his search for hidden money.

His flagging hopes rose as Sven rallied and made a brief attempt to speak.

"What is it old man? Need something?" Perhaps his uncle would make a deathbed bequest.

"Nothing. I'm not long for it now. Gonna join up with Sonja, soon. Ah, Sonja…she was the best thing that ever happened to me. Sonja, your mother…she loved you. The hardest thing she ever did was leave you with your father. You gotta know that, my boy. You have to know that."

Karl reached over and took his uncle's hand in his. He loved the old man more than he'd ever loved his father. "I know. I know. Rest, now. I'm here with you. I'm here."

As Karl's eyes scanned the nooks and crannies in the space above the stove, Sven breathed his last. It was over. The last member of his family had passed on. Tears slid down Karl's cheeks as he reached over, closing the cloudy eyes.

He stood up. Dragging a chair over to the stove, he climbed up on it. Reaching his hand up beside the stovepipe, he felt in a shallow space beside the rusting metal. Success. His fingers grasped a slender tin. Failure. Seven hundred dollars. That would get him as far as Winnipeg. He was going to Fiji.

◇◇◇◇◇◇

The seas swirled and struck against the ragged rocks showering rivulets of salt water over the spray zone mosses. As each wave subsided, another gathered in the channel waiting for its turn. Mesmerized by the ebb and flow, Karl sat in quiet contemplation.

He was satisfied with his uncle's burial site. The old guy would have been pleased with its location. After unexpectedly coming across Sonja's grave on a gentle hilltop, Karl dug Sven's grave beside it. A simple wooden cross adorned the mound and faced out towards the open ocean. Karl was unsure just how religious Sven had been, but the cross seemed appropriate. It marked the final resting place of this pioneering Swede.

The evening was quite warm for the beginning of April. Karl pulled on a sweater and continued to sit on his perch gazing towards his childhood homestead. He wondered about the family that had bought the place. On several occasions, he and his uncle had seen smoke rising from the site indicating the family was still there. Sven had told him about the visit from Sam and how he hadn't let the stranger come ashore. It was plain that his uncle had actively discouraged visitors of any kind preferring his solitude after Sonja's death.

He rose and strode quickly back to the cabin. Starting at one corner of the dingy home, he moved and shook pots, pans and tins; thumped walls; dismantled furniture and lifted the heavy stone grate under the stove. He scoured every last inch.

Shifting to the outbuildings, he systematically destroyed the decaying structures. He found nothing. By this time, darkness shrouded the ruined homestead. Karl had to give up the search for now.

Karl stuffed the lukewarm stew into his mouth, washing it down with the dregs of his whisky. Sighing, he checked the liquor stash. The light from the kerosene lantern reflected off three remaining bottles. With the spring storms now past, the weather was improving. It was time he was moving on.

Staring at the torn-apart building, Karl remembered the quiet orderliness of his childhood homestead. His father had kept the yard and gardens immaculate and his mother had been fastidious with her housekeeping. It was a far cry from this place. There was nothing to keep him here. Sven was dead. He was now certain the money either had never existed or was gone. The seven hundred dollars in a cigar tin was probably the last of it. *Where was the money? The brothers had made a fortune in the gold fields. Where was the money?*

He roared with laughter as he realized where it was; where it had been all along.

CHAPTER 28

SARA GLANCED OVER AT MARY WHO WAS STRUGGLING TO MAKE sense of the latest physics problem. She had tried to help, but had only succeeded in confusing her sister even more. Physics was neither of their strong points. "Give over for now. Let's have tea."

Mary shoved the notebook to one side and went to fill the kettle from the pail beside the door. They still kept the water bucket inside even though all danger of freezing had long passed. Spring was rapidly coming to their little patch of land. With it came the promise that Dad would be arriving soon.

"All we have left of the real tea is Earl Grey or some of that English Breakfast. Which do you want? Heavens, we'll soon be drinking the berry stuff. No lift in that," Mary complained.

Sara laughed. "Sure hope Dad or the supply boat comes before we are down to berry tea. Who do you think will be here first, Dad or Jennifer and Steve?"

Sara sat sipping her tea, reflecting on the way their winter had passed. The season had come and gone with surprising swiftness. Early on she and Mary had decided that routine was the best anti-dote for the endless waiting for their father.

Each morning after outside chores had been finished; time was set aside for school work. While Mary studied, Sara would paint or help her sister.

Mary had done well with her studies. Most of the assignments were finished and waiting for the next boat to take them into port to be posted on to the correspondence branch.

After lunch any further cooking and cleaning would be done, leaving plenty of time for them to immerse themselves in one of the many books that lined the shelves of their parents' room. Soon it would be time for evening chores, supper and bed.

Those were the good days. Other days had passed like molasses. The days when Mary lapsed into her lonely world were hell. Shaking her head, Sara turned her thoughts to more pleasant ones.

Yes, most days had passed quickly enough. Now that spring was coming, more outdoor work needed to be done. Sara mentally planned the garden. Would they need to plant before dad came back? She wondered if they would stay on. Where would they go, if they didn't?

◇◇◇◇◇◇

Mary watched Sara absentmindedly stirring her tea. A chill stole across her shoulders as she thought about the winter months. The time had been long, bleak and lonely. School work had been hard and she didn't see the use for it. She wasn't going back to the city even if Sara and Dad decided it was for the best.

She shuddered as she remembered the wolves surrounding their billy goat. The wolves had been waiting their chance. They had found the goat in the outside pen on the first day the girls had let him out in early spring. Again and again, the wolves had lunged and struck at the cornered creature.

It had taken Sara forever to load the shotgun. Finally, with one horrific blast, she had scattered the pack. Their goat was left bleeding in the churned snow. Day after day, the girls nursed the goat back to health. He limped badly now and his once proud face was a mass of scars.

Since then, her nightmares had become more hideous. Now, Sharon's images transformed from human to cougar to wolf...each with blood dripping... always Samuel's arms reaching out.

Sometimes when Mary looked in the mirror, she caught sight of the goat's scarred face with its fur matted into a reddish birthmark. This blurring of dreams and reality often drove her to shut down. She would wrap up Anna's quilt and sit swaying in the old rocker beside the stove. Eventually, the warmth from the fire would soothe her racing mind.

◇◇◇◇◇◇

Occasionally, even Sara had nightmares. She dreamt of Mary's open mouth calling silently to her as she struggled futilely to untangle the kelp binding her feet. It had been Mary who had triumphed that day. Mary had succeeded in releasing her from the seaweed. She had dragged Sara towards the surface. Mary had saved her life. She always woke with renewed determination. Maybe she couldn't save her sister from the sea, but she would protect her from bullies and the outside world. She had promised her father.

"Come on, let's get to the chores," Sara said as she tipped the dregs of her tea down the sink. "Any leftovers for the chickens?" She grabbed the slop bucket and rushed out the door.

◇◇◇◇◇◇

"Ahoy there. Hello"

Startled, the girls looked up to see a man standing on their dock. How long had he been there? They had been so intent on their chores that he had managed to land without their knowing it. The sisters stared at the intruder. Cautiously, they turned as one and began to walk towards their dock.

◇◇◇◇◇◇

Karl waited as both girls had made their way down to the rough wooden wharf. He took in their worn clothing, disheveled hair and rubber booted feet. He saw that one of them was hanging back shyly. Both were quite pretty with their long blonde hair and wide eyes. The shy one had some kind of wound covering half of her face. Although she tried to shield her cheek from his gaze, he saw that the wound was really a large disfiguring birthmark.

Sara smiled and held out her hand. "Hello."

Karl took her hand and shook it solemnly. "I'm Karl Thoresen. This used to be my home when I was a kid."

"Thoresen. Yes, that sounds familiar. We bought the homestead through a real estate firm, but I remember the owner had been a Thoresen. Must have been your parents."

"Actually it was me. My dad passed on that year and I had no wish to ever come back to live on the coast, so I sold the place. I remember meeting two young girls at the time. Couldn't have been you, could it?" He waited while the sisters absorbed the information.

Sara stared at the handsome man standing on their dock. "Must have been. I don't recall you, but I imagine we've all changed in the last few years. I'm so sorry about your father. It must be difficult for you to see the homestead again?" Sara looked at him with sympathy etched in her blue eyes. It was clear that the girl had taken an immediate liking to him.

Karl shuffled his feet and allowed his eyes to tear up. "Thanks, it is a bit. Still, that was a few years ago. Time does have a way of easing the pain of losing him. Cancer took him." He glanced seaward for a moment and then cleared his throat. "I just wanted to see the place one last time. I was over to see Sven on the island and thought I'd stop by."

Karl didn't see any reason to mention the old guy's death. He watched the last reservations leave the girls. He knew he'd gained their trust.

"Well, you'd best come up then. We've changed the place quite a bit since we got here. It was very run down and the woods were starting to take over." Sara motioned to Karl to follow her to the cabin. Mary hung back.

"Sara," she whispered. "I need to go for a walk." It was their code for when Mary felt overwhelmed by visitors. With those words she strode off towards the trail that led to the cave.

"Don't mind her," Sara said to Karl as they made their way to the cabin. "She's not keen on strangers. She'll come back when she feels more comfortable."

◇◇◇◇◇◇

Sara welcomed the new arrival. She had been so lonely over the winter. It was so nice to have company, especially someone who had grown up here on the homestead. Showing Karl all the improvements to the buildings, the new water system and the recently cleared meadow gave her much pleasure. She chatted cheerfully, relaxing into her new-found friendship.

Karl appeared interested in all she had to show him. He seemed clearly impressed by the changes he saw in the old homestead. It was obvious that the Lindholms intended to make this their home for many years to come.

"My goodness, what a clever system," he exclaimed as Sara went over the intricate details of building and maintaining the water system. "My mother would have loved this. Dad never got around to running water. We had to trudge up that hill to the creek in all kinds of weather. Many a time I lost most of the water in the bucket from slipping on the muddy trail."

Sara laughed at the mental image of Karl sliding down the hill covered in dirt and leaves.

Karl smiled to himself. *Yes, the Thoresen charm was working. He'd have these girls eating out of his hand in no time.*

Sara suddenly realized that it was getting late; too late for Karl to venture back to Thoresen Island that day. "It's getting quite dark. In fact, it's probably already too dark for you to head back over. I can make us some supper and you could go in the morning. Will your uncle worry if you don't go back tonight?"

"No, he won't worry. I didn't want to spoil our day, but he died two weeks ago and I buried him next to Mom. I just stopped in to see this place on my way back to the mainland. Lost Sven to cancer. Same way as my Dad."

"Oh, gosh, I'm so sorry for you." Sara reached out and touched Karl's arm.

He shrugged and straightened his shoulders. "That's life. He was in his eighties but I really miss the old bugger."

Skittering rocks betrayed Mary's decent down the hillside. They looked up to see her coming towards them. The hood of her sweatshirt partially covered her face, but she was smiling.

"Hey, Mary. I've just been showing Karl all the changes since he was here last. He's going to come in for supper with us. It will be nice to have company."

Mary shrugged and nodded her head. "Let's have a fish fry. We could use the salmon I caught yesterday. That and some fiddlehead ferns if you'll pick them. Rice would be nice, but we don't have much of that left."

"Well, you're in luck, Mary. I've got a whole bag of brown rice on the boat." With that Karl sped off down to his boat to retrieve his contribution to supper.

◇◇◇◇◇◇

Whistling happily to himself, he marvelled how fortunate he was. Not only did he have access to his old homestead, where he was sure his father had hidden money, but he'd found some new female companions. With a little luck he'd have himself bed, board and money.

For several days, Karl kept his distance and did not become too familiar with the sisters. Sure, he spent a lot of time talking, laughing and joking, but he made sure that at the end of the day he wandered off to his boat to sleep. He could see that Sara was at ease with his company, but Mary still kept to herself. She often disappeared and when she was with them, she kept the left side of her face turned resolutely away from him.

Over time, Sara let it slip that they'd been waiting all winter for their father to return from fishing. He had been horrified when he heard of how the mother had died. In all his years at this home-stead, he'd never even seen a cougar. He marvelled at how Sara and Mary had kept it together surviving the long winter by themselves. Gradually, he broached the subject of Mary's weird behaviour.

Sara sighed. Over several cups of berry tea, she outlined the torment that Mary had suffered in high school. "She seemed to be so much better off here on the homestead...that is until the cougar killed Mom and Samuel. Now, she often retreats into herself for hours at a time. It's as though she goes to a secret world in her mind where she feels safe. There's no telling what will set her off. Sometimes, she knows a spell is coming and will just go off by herself or she'll wrap up in Mom's old quilt and sit by the stove. Other times, that mental door slams so quickly that I can see the light fading from her eyes. Those times are the longest...they can last for days."

"My God, that must be rough on you. There's no one to help. That must be hell."

"Worse for her, I imagine. She did try to tell me about some of her dreams once, but that telling brought on a shutdown that lasted almost four days. Now, we just don't talk about it. When she returns from 'away', we just act like nothing happened."

"Christ," muttered Karl. He had even more respect for Sara's ability to cope here, alone. He found that very attractive. She was much like him. He changed the subject. "Best we start milking that goat of yours. She's bleating up a storm out there."

CHAPTER 29

MARY FELT A COLD CHILL STEAL AROUND HER HEART. SHE watched Sara tilt her face towards Karl, as she laughed at one of his jokes. She knew her sister was very attracted to this handsome stranger and she didn't blame her. There was something about Karl's charming ways that had even succeeded in melting some of her reservations. It hurt, though, to see Sara becoming such good friends with someone else. *Where would that leave her?* Guilt flooded through her as she remembered she was to blame for their isolation. *Sara deserved happiness. Sara deserved to find someone to care for. But where would that leave her?*

Unable to deal with her conflicting emotions, Mary left the cabin to start digging over the garden patch. It would soon be time for planting and they couldn't wait much longer. Dad would expect the vegetables to be started by the beginning of June, at the latest.

"Here, let me do that. I need to make myself useful around here." Karl stood in front of her with his hand out for the hoe. "You ladies have been feeding me like royalty since I came. Here, give me that hoe."

◇◇◇◇◇◇

Karl made short work of the vegetable patch and enlarged it by at least five feet on the south side. He relished in the physical work, feeling the muscles in his back and arms strengthening as he worked the land. He despised those people who allowed themselves to become unfit. With all the troubles he'd been in, he was proud he could at least defend himself in a fair fight. He shook his head as he remembered why he was on the run. Right now, he knew he was safe, but there was no telling when someone would see him here at the homestead. The Kingdom Army's reach was wide. Unless he disappeared overseas, he'd never be secure. He spat as he thought of the Army and its long tentacles. Yes, they could reach anywhere even to this remote patch of the West Coast.

He knew it was time to be moving on. He'd been with the girls for almost three weeks. Karl began planning his next moves.

Karl entered the cabin with a flourish. With much fanfare, he produced a bottle of whiskey from behind his back. "Ladies, it's time for a toast. It's my birthday."

Mary and Sara looked up from making supper. "Oh no, you should have told us! We could have baked a cake or something," Sara said in dismay. "Everyone needs a cake to celebrate."

"No need. It's only my thirtieth. Getting to be an old man, I am," joked Karl as he found three glasses in the cupboard. "You ladies going to join me or do I have to drink alone?"

Sara stole a quick glance at Mary. They were not at all used to drinking. Once in a while they had been allowed to have a small glass of wine at Christmas, but that had been before they'd come to the homestead. Still, Sara felt it might be rude not to toast someone's birthday. Smiling she turned to Karl and said, "Sure, we'll have a small toast."

As Karl made them a weak whiskey and water, she whispered to Mary. "Just a bit won't hurt us."

Turning to Karl, she raised her glass. "Happy birthday to our new friend. May you enjoy many more."

The girls quickly made a sticky toffee pudding and placed one of the emergency candles in the center of it. The resulting birthday cake was hilarious. The candle, when lit, tilted at a crazy angle and rose like a phoenix spreading flickering shadows over the dim cabin. Laughter erupted and the party was on. The sisters shared the Lindholm' tradition of telling the birthday person's fortune and even played a couple of songs on their flutes. Not to be outdone, Karl retrieved his guitar from his boat and began to serenade the ladies.

As several glasses of whiskey were enjoyed, the trio grew quieter. Thoughts were cast backwards into the past. Mary grew solemn and pleaded a headache. She stole off to bed leaving Sara and Karl hunched over the table deep in conversation.

"You are such a good listener, Sara," Karl said placing his hand over hers. "I feel I can tell you anything, even the shame that led to Sven leaving this homestead."

Sara looked into his eyes and whispered, "Of course you can. You can tell me anything. I told you about Mary's problems and you haven't judged us. I'll listen."

Karl allowed his eyes to well and then in small halting stages he told of Sven and his mother's betrayal of Harry, his father. Pausing several times for effect, he painted a picture of a young boy being abandoned by his mother and abused by a revengeful father. He wove a tale of regret and heartache. He told her how Sven had told him on his deathbed that his mother had always loved him.

Gazing at Sara in the lamplight, he permitted a small sob to escape his lips. "I have nothing to remember her by. I know she kept a little bit of jewelry hidden here at the cabin. She didn't have time to take it with her when they left for the island, so it must still be here somewhere. You didn't find a silver necklace with a cameo pendant when you were fixing the place up did you?"

"No, we didn't find anything. It could still be around here some place. We cleaned and fixed the holes in the roof, but that's about all we did to the cabin. We did build that partition."

"It would mean so much to have that necklace. Maybe someday I could give it to a soul mate or lover." Karl squeezed Sara's hand.

Sara felt warmth rising to her cheeks. Quickly she brushed aside those feelings and became practical. "Well, starting first thing in the morning, we should go on your treasure hunt. If it's here, we'll find it. Now, it's time you were heading down to the boat. I have to get some sleep. The chores are only a couple of hours away." She walked with him to the door.

Karl, unwilling to press his luck, gave her a quick hug and left.

Sara stood for a long time in the open doorway watching Karl make his way to the boat. Unfamiliar feelings crept through her body as she relived his embrace.

◇◇◇◇◇◇

While they did their morning chores, Sara filled Mary in on what Karl had told her after she'd gone to bed. "I feel so sorry for him. To have his mother leave him like that and then to find out she regretted it to her dying day. Let's do our best to find those jewels."

Mary's eyes reflected the sympathy in Sara's heart. "There weren't any boxes or hidden jewels when we fixed this place up. We would have found them. You know how we scrubbed every inch of this cabin and more. Sara, I bet it's in the cave somewhere. I'll look there and you guys can search around here."

"Good idea. We can help you later, when we get done with the cabin and out buildings."

"No. Let me do the cave alone. I don't want Karl prying around my special place. I don't want him in there." There was an underlying firmness to Mary's voice. Her fists clenched and she started to tense.

"No worries. I will keep him away from your hidey-hole. I can see how you want to keep it to yourself. Don't worry," promised Sara eager to ward off any potential shutdown. That's the last thing she needed. Mary had been quite good for the last while.

◇◇◇◇◇◇

Throughout the morning Sara and Karl searched the buildings. A couple of small tins were found. One contained candles and matches and the other held some seeds that Anna had squirreled away for the next year's planting.

They increased their search pattern to include the dock and even around the creek. Towards evening, they had to give up for the day. Mary joined them at the plank table. Karl had brought out the whiskey again.

"No thanks," said the girls in unison when he offered them a shot.

"Last night was special. It was your birthday. We don't usually drink. It's not that wise when you are by yourself and your nearest neighbour is miles away. If someone gets hurt, you need all your wits about you." Sara pushed the bottle away.

Karl shrugged and poured himself a double.

"Did you get that cave done, Mary?" he asked looking directly at the younger sister. "I can just see my mother tucking something in beside the preserves or in the bottom of an onion bin."

"Nothing in there, I'm afraid. I turned the place inside out. I did find this, though." She placed a long thin box, similar to the box he'd found in beside Sven's chimney, on the table.

Karl tried to keep the excitement from showing on his face.

"Anything in it?"

"Just some old money. No necklace, I'm afraid."

"Oh, slide it over here and let's count it." Karl reached for the tin and pried open the lid.

The girls watched as he counted out over five hundred dollars. "Not bad. I wonder if there is more where this came from."

"No, that's the only box in there. I searched really well, especially after I found this one."

Karl casually slid the money towards Sara. "Nice little nest egg for you gals," he said. "Now what's for supper, my ladies? Fish stew or fish fry?" They often joked about how much fish they ate. The venison that Anna had cured had long been eaten and neither girl had fancied shooting any of the small deer that occasionally rambled through their place.

◇◇◇◇◇◇◇

That night after Karl had wandered back down to his boat, the girls discussed what to do with the money. Five hundred dollars was quite a bit and would come in handy for the next batch of supplies. Still, the supplies were paid out of the trust money their parents had put aside. Dad had arranged for the store to withdraw the payment automatically. It saved a lot of hassle and the merchant didn't have to wait for his money.

"Maybe we should split it with Karl?" suggested Sara. "You found it, but it was his dad or mom's money in the first place." After much discussion, it was decided to split the money three ways. They would tell Karl in the morning.

◇◇◇◇◇◇

Meanwhile Karl lay in his bunk occasionally peeking out of the tiny porthole to see if the light was still on in the cabin. The dim light vanished. The girls had gone to bed.

Stealthily Karl crept along the path, past the cabin and up to the cave. His flashlight illuminated the cave's entrance. There it was just as he remembered from his childhood. The entrance was almost hidden by the overgrown brush. Sweeping aside the low cedar branches, he bent down low and infiltrated Mary's sanctuary.

Quickly he sorted through the rows of preserves, the potato sacks, and the onion and squash bins. He found nothing. He replaced each item carefully. Turning around slowly, he examined the rest of the room. It seemed as though Mary had made herself quite a nest. A small bed had been made from an old wooden pallet and a sleeping bag. A flask of water and some dried fruit lay on a shelf beside the bed. An ancient oil lamp rested against the wall. Another shelf held an assortment of books and papers.

Sensing rather than hearing a presence, Karl spun towards the cave opening to stare at the crouching figure.

Mary's face shone with fury. "I told you there was nothing here. Get out." He rushed by her, making for the entrance.

As he passed, he watched her eyes turn cold.

"Get out."

He fled toward his boat cursing himself for being so bloody careless. Now Mary would be suspicious of him. He already could see that she was becoming jealous of his and Sara's budding relationship. This would only add to her mistrust. She'd tell Sara he'd been ransacking the cave. Neither would be happy. Now, they'd be watching his every move. *Damn.*

The next morning Karl sauntered into the cabin as usual. Sara was sitting alone stirring her tea.

"Mary's in one of her times," she said. "She left for the cave in the middle of the night and hasn't been back. I'll go up later and see her. Not much point going right now." Sara rose and ladled out some porridge into bowls for Karl and herself. Silently they spooned the comforting food into their mouths.

"Saw her climbing up the hill when I went to the outhouse," Karl said. "I called to her, but she just gave fright and carried on. Doubt if she'll even remember she saw me."

"Most times she forgets what happens while she's in a state. Things get all mixed up in her mind." Sara's shoulders began to shake.

Karl crossed over to her quickly and put his arms around her. Drawing her into a warm embrace, he simply held her while she cried unstoppable tears.

Eventually the weeping ceased and Sara moved away. "I'd better go see to her. Can you milk Daisy and feed the chickens for me?"

"Sure, no problem."

Sara left and Karl set about the chores worrying what Mary might be saying to Sara. He decided that if Sara questioned him, his best course of action was to simply deny going into the cave. Knowing how fragile Mary's memories were, Sara would have no trouble believing him over her sister.

He did not have to worry.

Sara came back very quickly. "She's sound asleep in her little bed in there. When she's like this, she can sleep most of the day."

"Alright, my girl. Then you and I will have a little vacation from all of this. She's safe enough and it is a beautiful day. Let's take a picnic up on top of the cliff. I bet we could see for miles today."

◇◇◇◇◇◇

Sara smiled. It was time she had a little fun for herself. A picnic on top of the cliff would be far better than hanging around the cabin all day, worrying about Mary. He was right, Mary was safe and she usually slept for hours. These episodes exhausted her so much that when she did come back from the cave, she usually went straight to her bed in the cabin. "You're right, she'll be fine. I'll fix us up a bit of lunch and we can be back before supper."

As they climbed the hill, their cares seemed to be carried away on the stiff ocean breeze. The view from on top, indeed, stretched for miles. Today, the ocean was a shimmering jewel flashing blue and green in the sunlight. Gulls wheeled overhead, their cries competing with the crash of the surf on the rocks below.

Sara carefully spread Anna's bright blue tablecloth. She loved that spread as it brought back happy memories of her mother. Blue had been her mother's favorite colour. A brief shadow flitted through her mind as she remembered that it was also the colour of the housedress that Anna had worn when the cougar had killed Samuel. Determined to make the best of this lovely day, Sara emptied the picnic basket and beckoned to Karl to join her.

Karl had brought his last bottle of merlot to add to the picnic. He uncorked it with a flourish.

They relaxed into easy company. Few words were needed as they sat sipping the warm wine and munching goat cheese and pickle sandwiches. Afterwards, they lay back luxuriating in the strength of the late spring sun.

Karl's arms drew Sara into a close embrace. He became a little bolder and easing his hand up her t-shirt. She murmured soft words of encouragement. He rolled over her and began to explore further.

◇◇◇◇◇◇

Mary kept cycling through horrific dreams and semi-awareness. The cool underground atmosphere competed with the white hot anger generated by Karl invading her space, leaving her unable to completely escape into her mind. She tossed restlessly on the narrow pallet.

She relived the beating in the stairwell. She recalled the callous, cruel barbs that pierced her soul. Sharon's harsh laughter, the stench of urine and damp, the sickening odour of cheap Dollar Store perfume and the sharp concrete scraping against her back as she slid down the wall, all came hurtling back into her mind. Then the hideous sight of Anna's blue dress drenched in blood melded with the vision of her mother's arms around the scarcely recognizable shape that had been her baby brother. She could hear the sounds of wolves growling as they tortured her helpless goat. She watched Sara's frantic hands shake as she struggled to load the gun. Her mouth fell open in shock as the thunderous blast of the shot reverberated in her memory.

Mary couldn't burrow down far enough or wrap up tightly enough in the sleeping bag to ease the pain. Her usual comforts failed. The cold fingers of damp finally drove her from the cave. With her eyes tearing in the sunlight, Mary staggered out along the path towards the cliff face. Perhaps there, she could breathe.

Squinting against the harsh glare, she stumbled over roots, rocks and shale as she made her way along the trail. Gasping with effort, she slowed, sinking to her knees. She tried to corral her spiralling thoughts. As she forced herself to take small shallow breaths, Mary heard sounds dancing on the breeze.

Anna was laughing as she played with Samuel.

The sweet echoes drew her to her feet and she ran eagerly towards the sounds. "Mom…"

Freezing in horror, Mary watched as the cougar crouched over her mother. She could hear the snarling and biting as it ripped into her mother; staining the blue dress red. A white leg poked out from beneath the tawny body.

Desperately, Mary looked around for a weapon. Seizing a large spruce bough, she raised it over her head. Vibrations rippled in the hushed air. Solid thwacks shattered the now silent scene.

The cougar turned its head and Karl gaped at his attacker.

Mary stared as Karl slowly got to his feet and staggered towards her, his body lurching as he reached out to defend himself. He was shoving her down into the dirt, his hands grabbing at the branch. "You crazy cow-faced bitch," he snarled. "What in hell are you doing? Crazy bitch!" He tossed the branch away and reached around her neck trying to choke the life out of her.

Suddenly, Mary felt a crushing heaviness as Karl fell forward. She watched his face crumple. Blood spattered everywhere.

Once more, Sara brought the huge rock smashing against his skull. A final blow and Karl lay like a pile of rags and bone.

Mary rolled from underneath the bruising weight. "Oh, my God, Sara. I thought it was the cougar. I thought it was the cougar attacking Mom. It was Karl. Is he…"

"Dead? Oh God, Mary I don't know. He was hurting you…I had to save you," screamed Sara as she took in the scene before her. "What have I done?"

Blood pooled under Karl's head, soaking the dusty path. Sara sank to her knees. She carefully turned him over. Empty lifeless eyes rolled back in his head as a final gurgle hissed its way from Karl's throat. A primordial wail shredded the sea breeze as Sara understood the finality of it all.

The sisters crouched beside Karl's body. Moments turned into minutes and minutes evolved into eternity. Finally, Sara turned to her sister. "What are we going to do? He's dead. We've killed him. We've murdered him."

"No. We didn't. I was the one who hit first. You just tried to save me."

"Who'd believe us? They'll take us away, back to the mainland. I'll go to jail and there won't be anyone to look after you. I promised Dad I'd take care of you. I promised Dad."

Sara rose resolutely to her feet. "We have to get rid of him."

Mary simply stared at Sara. Her eyes clouding over as she began sinking into oblivion.

"No, Mary," begged Sara. "Don't leave me now. Help me do this." She yanked Mary's hair and forced her sister to look at her. "I can't do this alone. Help me, Mary. You have to."

Wooden words tumbled from Mary's lips. "The crevasse. Put him in the crevasse."

The sisters took hold of Karl's battered body. Dragging it up and over the small rise, they positioned it on the edge of the fissure. Together they shoved the carcass into the hole. They heard rocks dislodging as the body tumbled its way to the water level. Peering over the edge, they saw that it had become wedged beside the old deer bones. Crabs would make short work of any flesh and with luck the bones would either wash away or blend in with the deer skeleton. Karl was gone.

Sara looked at Mary. All reserves had been stripped away leaving a hollow shell moving robotically. Mary had disappeared. She took her sister's arm and led her away.

As the nightmares reigned, Mary screamed and cursed throughout the long night. When dawn approached she fell silent. She sat motionless in the rocker, staring into space.

◇◇◇◇◇◇

Alone, Sara grieved for Karl. He had been a glimpse of what could have been hers if she wasn't marooned on this homestead. When their father came back she might be able to leave and pursue a dream of a husband and lover, perhaps a family of her own. For now, she was a prisoner in the wilderness. They had a deadly secret that could never be told.

Mary had left the cabin later that morning to seek the solace of her sanctuary. She had been holed up there for over three weeks. Sara had taken to leaving food just inside the entrance. Sometimes it was eaten, but more often, it grew mouldy and stale.

On one visit, Sara had been successful in getting her sister to talk about what had happened, but it was obvious that Mary blamed herself for Karl's death. During her latest state, she had convinced herself that she alone was to blame for Karl's death. She talked about ending it all. She said she would leave a written confession, absolving Sara of any blame. No amount of explaining could persuade Mary to accept the truth. They were both responsible for killing Karl. She would have to keep Mary from talking to anyone until their father returned. He'd know what to do. Mary couldn't be trusted anymore.

"Mary, Mary," Sara called softly to her sister. She could see Mary crouched on an upturned crate. "Come down to the cabin with me and I'll make us some tea. We'll sit on the bench and see if we can see any boats coming. You want to see if Dad's coming, don't you?"

The only response was some shuffling of feet and the strange high-pitched hum that Mary used to comfort herself.

Sara turned slowly away from the entrance. It was no use.

For the first time since the incident, Sara forced herself to return to the cliff path. She tried to avoid the crevasse, but it drew her like a magnet. She knelt and peered into the chasm. Waves echoed as they advanced and retreated in the narrow opening.

Over the last few weeks, there had been no storms or rough seas. As she watched the wave action, she caught sight of the body. Shuddering, she saw that the water and sea life were making short work of it. Dark wet clothing eddied around greyish-green bones. Soon little would remain, but the heavier bones. Sara wasn't too worried about anyone finding them since the crevasse was so very well camouflaged. Eventually, Karl's bones would blend in with those of the deer skeleton.

She realized, however, that she had to erase all traces of Karl's visit to their homestead. No one had come by while he was here, but his boat was still tied to the dock. It hadn't rained so there might still be blood at the picnic site. Steeling herself, she continued up the trail.

Spread out before her were the remainders of their idyllic picnic. Animals had rooted through the food. The half empty wine bottle still lay propped up against the basket. Large spatters of blood had darkened the bright blue table cloth. A large pool of dried caked blood stained the soil. A bloodied branch and smeared rock completed the incriminating evidence. Her stomach roiled. Sara turned her head away. She couldn't believe they were responsible for this carnage.

Doggedly, she broke the bottom off the wine bottle and began digging under a nearby nursery log. It was easy enough work, but it took her ages to scrape a hole big enough to hold the basket, table cloth and picnic supplies. Brushing the dirt off her hands, she began scraping the encrusted blood away from the path. She hurled the branch and rock off the cliff into the surf. Satisfied that the wind and eventual rain would erase any other traces from the scene, Sara stoically returned to the cave and once again tried to coax her sister to come out.

Mary simply spoke one word. "Soon."

◇◇◇◇◇◇◇

The cabin door opened and Mary crept inside. Crossing over to her sister's bed, she slipped under the covers reaching for Sara's comforting arms. Holding on to the familiar warmth, she allowed herself to be reassured. *Sara was her one constant. Sara would look after her.*

CHAPTER 30

OVER THE NEXT FEW DAYS, SARA SET UP THEIR NEW ROUTINE. Breakfast was followed by outside chores. Then, she encouraged Mary to do a couple of hours school work while she worked on her latest painting. In the afternoon, she encouraged Mary to nap while she fished or worked on the vegetable patch. Each evening, the sisters sat on the bench looking out to sea watching for any sign of their father coming home. Sara understood how important it was for Mary to have a schedule and shape to her day. Her sister's mind was so fragile that any deviation from their pattern caused stress and the threat of another withdrawal.

Sara also knew that she had to get rid of the boat. As the weather warmed and the seas remained calm, it was only a matter of time before the Coast Guard called in on one of their patrols. She was looking forward to seeing Jennifer and Steven again, but Karl's boat was a huge problem. Although she thought he had been travelling without firm plans, she couldn't be sure. By now, some relative or friends may have reported Karl overdue and missing.

Finally, after Mary had dropped off to sleep one night, Sara made her way down to the dock. Using the light from her hurricane lamp, she searched through Karl's things. His ship's papers were in the name of a Fredrick Morton. She couldn't find any license for the radio. His knapsack held various odds and ends including some cards and several sets of contact lenses. She did find a long tin box and two handguns hidden under the mattress. Prying open the silver tin revealed several hundred dollars in musty old bills. As Sara counted the money and examined the weapons, she slowly came to terms with the fact that Karl was not who he had pretended to be. Her heart pounded as she realized that there was more to Karl's circumstances than he had allowed them to know. A false identity, money and guns indicated criminal activity.

Quickly she gathered all the food, equipment and batteries that she could find. She shoved it all in a duffel bag that she'd unearthed from under the bunk. There was no point in wasting stuff they could use. Sara knew she had to get rid of the boat.

Prowling around the deck, she found several gas cans. Two were full. Hauling the loaded duffel bag ashore, Sara went back to the cabin. Thankfully, Mary was still asleep and she was able to hide her booty under her parents' bed. She carefully crept into her bed. Lying quietly, unable to sleep, she plotted how she was going to get rid of the last piece of evidence that could tie them to Karl.

The next night as the moon illuminated the slack sea, Sara eased her way into the icy cold water. Barnacled rocks made it impossible for her to remove her waterlogged sneakers. Clumsily she manoeuvered over slippery seaweed covered rocks, nearly falling up to her waist in the frigid sea. Pain radiated up her leg as her ankle twisted. With the cold numbing her feet, she waded on determined to make it round the point. The current was getting stronger threatening to rip the boat's painter from her wet hands. Her feet were swept out from underneath her. Frantically, she held on to the rope as she scrabbled to regain her footing. Twisting her body around, she knelt awkwardly scraping her bare knees on the gritty encrusted rocks. This was far enough. This would have to do.

Tying the sodden rope around the closest boulder, she knelt in the dark ocean. Willing her frozen feet to hold her weight, she stood and grasped the boat's railing. Using the last of her energy, she clambered aboard. *Just a few minutes more and it will be finished.*

Dragging herself along the railing, Sara made her way to the stern. She shook each gas can she came to until she found the two full ones. She doused the deck and wheelhouse. She soaked the steps leading down into the cabin. Satisfied, Sara looked around and collected some oil soaked rags. After stuffing them into her jacket, she climbed overboard and eased herself over the rocks. Her hands shook as she struggled to set the rags on fire. Eventually they flared; burning quickly. She had barely enough time to toss them aboard. As flames engulfed the deck, Sara untied the painter setting Karl's boat adrift.

As she stood watching, the current caught the drifting boat and took it out past the point and on towards Thoresen Island. The flames careened across the fuel soaked deck reaching the engines. The ensuing explosions rent the night sky. Sara turned and headed for home. She had sealed their fate. They were at the mercy of the wilderness until their father returned.

◇◇◇◇◇◇

Steven and his new partner, James, threw grappling hooks over the railing of the burned out cabin cruiser, drawing it up beside the Coast Guard cutter.

"Looks like this boat is a write-off. Can you read the registration?" James asked.

Steven leaned over the side of their boat, straining to read the scorched numbers on the hull. "No, not enough left to ID. Too much damage to risk boarding. We'd go through the deck for sure."

"Well, we can't leave it floating. It is a hazard. Let's tow it into that cove and beach it. Maybe we should call that salvage outfit in Rupert." James threw the cutter's engine into low gear and the tow was underway.

◇◇◇◇◇◇

Two weeks later, Sara's heart sank as she identified the approaching vessel as the Coast Guard cutter. It was not their father. "Mary,

Coast Guard is coming. We talked about this. Get up to the cave and I'll let you know if it is Jennifer and Steven."

According to their plan, Mary was to stay out of sight if visitors came to the homestead. Sara had convinced her that the police knew Karl had disappeared and that they were looking for his killer. She told her sister that the only way she would be safe was to hide. Strangers wouldn't understand what had happened. "You know how you blurt things out. If they stare at your face you get stressed and sometimes you don't realize what you are saying. If you want to keep me from going to jail, you'll stay hidden. Okay."

"I wouldn't say it was you. I'd tell them the truth. I killed Karl."

"See what I mean. You'd tell and we would be caught. I know you think you killed him, but it was both of us. We'd never survive going to jail. The bullies in jail are worse than ten Sharons. I couldn't help you…we'd be separated and I promised Dad I'd protect you."

"I know, but…"

"No buts. We have to do this until Dad comes back and figures a way out of this mess. Go up to the cave. Stay there until I come and get you." She shoved Mary towards the trail. "Get going."

She pasted a smile on her face and went to greet her visitors. Steven's happy face was wreathed in smiles as he hugged Sara. "Where's my girl, Mary?" he said looking around for the younger sister.

Sara grimaced. "I'm afraid she's in one of her moods. Perhaps she'll come down later. Where's Jennifer? Is this a new partner?"

"Jennifer got married last week. She's been transferred to Vancouver. .. She said to say hi and to wish you well. This here's James…not nearly as pretty as Jen, but he'll have to do."

Over the course of the evening meal, Sara spun her tale of lies. She told Steven that their father had come home and had already returned to the fishing banks. "He is heartbroken about Mom and Samuel but he is determined to stay on here at the homestead. He says that's what she would have wanted."

"Is that what you want, Sara?"

"Yes, of course. Mary and I are happy here. You know she'd never be able to fit back into life in the city. She's too fragile. Maybe when she's older or gets better I will go to art school, but for now we'll stay put."

"Can you manage?" Steven looked deep into her eyes.

Uncomfortable, Sara looked away. "Yes, I can manage. Supplies are coming in on the next boat and Dad will be back again in a couple of months. He'll be back before winter." Her bright determined voice begged him to understand. "This is my choice. It's my life and I will live it the way I want. I have what's left of my family, my art and my memories of Mom and Samuel. This is my choice."

In the morning, Steven and James left on the outgoing tide. Steven was worried about the Lindholm sisters, but Sara was right. It was their choice where they lived. He had to respect that. Turning to give a last wave, Steven gave the cutter more fuel and headed towards Thoresen Island.

Sara went up to the cave. "All clear. You can come out now."

There was no answer. "It's okay. Company's gone." She ventured further into the underground cavern.

Mary was slumped against the wall.

"Mary…"

Mary sat up. Unintelligible speech tumbled from her lips. She seemed out of it.

Sara glanced around and saw the dregs of a drink in a cracked cup. On the cave floor was a prescription pill bottle. She snatched the vial up and read the label. Silenor…the drug the doctor had given Sam for insomnia, many years ago. There was no telling how much Mary had consumed.

"Get up, Mary. What did you do?" How much did you take?"

Mary turned her head and threw up all over Sara's sweatshirt.

Sara dragged her sister to the cave entrance and propped her up in the fresh air. Frantically, Sara tried to judge how many of the sleeping pills Mary might have taken. The bottle had initially contained 50 tablets and at least forty were left. Had her father used any? She had no idea. Was Mary using them just to drift into sleep or had she meant to kill herself?

After several anxious moments, Sara decided to force Mary to walk. Hauling her up by her sweater, she pushed her sister along in front of her. Several feet along the trail, Mary was sick again. Sara was relieved to see Mary begin to stand better and start to protest her mistreatment. She was improving.

"Stop, stop." Mary pushed feebly at Sara's hands. "I can walk. Leave me alone."

"What did you do? Where did you get the pills? Why did you take the pills?"

Mary turned and looked straight at her angry sister. "What are you on about? Why are you so mad?"

It was plain that Mary had no recollection of the last while. Rather than cause a shutdown, Sara simply took her in her arms and held her tightly.

"You must have eaten something that upset your stomach. Let's go down and get some tea."

Later that evening, Sara retrieved the vial of sleeping pills and took the rest of the medications from the first aid box. Although she knew now that she had to protect Mary from herself, she didn't want to destroy the drugs.

It was up to her to keep the two of them safe. Mary could easily overdose or unintentionally betray their secret. If Mary became resistant to hiding away when visitors came, she could slip her a small dose of Silenor to keep her quiet. She shook her head at her dark thoughts. *Where was her father? He must come home soon. She couldn't take much more.* Wrapping everything up in a small plastic bag, she slipped the drugs under an old straw bale in the goat shed.

CHAPTER 31

ON THURSDAY OF THE FOLLOWING WEEK, THE NATIVE FISH BOAT, the *Kiri,* came by with their half-yearly supplies. They brought news that the Korean boat had given up the supply contract and that they had been hired to do the twice yearly run.

"Do you have any news from the Korean boat? Have you heard how my dad is doing?" Sara peppered the crew with questions. Then she fell silent as she realized she might give away their plight if she asked anymore.

"No, don't know why they gave up the contract. Probably didn't pay enough. We come by here a lot so it's no trouble for us." The crew offloaded the goods onto the deck and shoved off. "See you, later, maybe on our return sweep."

Sara waved and soon she was left by herself staring out to sea.

She glanced through the mail that had come with the supplies. A long, thin envelope with a return address of McNeil and McFader stood out from the usual magazines and bills. It looked official. With trepidation, she tore open the envelope and withdrew a single page.

The terse form letter was informing Anna that her mother had been killed in a car crash in December of last year. It gave the basic facts of the accident and went on to say that the trust fund would continue to be held at the CIBC in Rupert. The family signing members, Anna, Sam and Sara could still withdraw funds and write cheques to the annual limit. When both girls, Sara and Mary, had reached their twenty-first birthday, they would have to decide what to do with the remaining monies.

As Sara refolded the letter, the news sank in. She had loved her feisty grandmother. Mabel had been very good to them. What a horrible way to die…in an accident. She sobbed as she realized that Mabel had not even known that Anna and Samuel were gone. Mary and Sara were waiting for their father to tell Mabel the sad news when he got back.

She remembered those days just before they left for the homestead. It had been a time filled with the promise of adventure and tinged with the sadness of parting. Now, she had to break the news to Mary.

As she gathered Mary into her arms, she whispered, "Remember Grandma Mabel…she's gone. There was a car accident and she died. She's now in heaven with Mom and Samuel. We never did get to tell her that Mom died. Perhaps that's just as well."

Mary let the news wash over her. "We're almost like Karl now. Only, we still have Dad. He had no one left."

Sara sat quietly for a while, letting her thoughts drift back in time. Sighing softly, she gently pushed Mary aside and went to fill the kettle. "Let's make those Chinese lanterns and say good-bye to Grandma. We could let them drift out to sea and say a little prayer."

Mary reached up and got the box of special paper from the kitchen shelf. "Perhaps Grandma will see the lanterns from heaven and think of us. I loved Grandma."

The next evening, the girls lit small candles and placed them in the lanterns they'd nailed to a flat piece of board. Mary pushed wood gently out on the waves. As the evening tide flowed, the lights were carried further and further away. Soon the twinkling candles were swallowed up by the darkness. "Goodbye, Grandma…goodbye," sobbed the girls as loneliness gripped them in its cold embrace.

◇◇◇◇◇◇

Sara dusted off her faded blue housedress and stood surveying a promising crop of carrots and turnips. They had done well. She knew the cave was full of produce, canning and dried fish. There had been no shortage of fish to catch this year. When Dad got home, they'd try for some of those small coastal deer that made such a nuisance of themselves. Until then, she knew there was plenty of fish and chicken. Funny, she didn't mind butchering chickens and bashing fish over the head, but killing the deer was quite another thing.

Suddenly chilled by the cooling air, she went to get Mary.

Mary was sitting in her usual spot on the old garden bench. She sat there most evenings watching as the sun sank behind Thoresen Island.

"Scoot over, Mary. Here's your sweater," she said placing the frayed garment around her sister's shoulders.

Darkness had come quickly, leaving the moon shining over the bay. They sat companionably, side by side, on the bench with their eyes scanning the darkening sea. With a quiet sigh, Sara reached over and touched her sister's silver hair. "Best we go in now. It doesn't look like he's coming, tonight."

CPSIA information can be obtained at www.ICGtesting.com
Printed in the USA
LVOW07s1245190815

450655LV00002B/80/P